Joseph Bennett

**Luigi Cherubini**

Joseph Bennett

**Luigi Cherubini**

ISBN/EAN: 9783337221683

Printed in Europe, USA, Canada, Australia, Japan

Cover: Foto ©Raphael Reischuk / pixelio.de

More available books at **www.hansebooks.com**

NOVELLO'S PRIMERS OF MUSICAL BIOGRAPHY.

# LUIGI CHERUBINI

BY

## JOSEPH BENNETT.

*PRICE ONE SHILLING.*

*LONDON & NEW YORK*
NOVELLO, EWER AND CO.

*May also be had cloth gilt, price Two Shillings.*

# EXTRACT FROM THE PROSPECTUS OF THE SERIES:—

"The intention of NOVELLO's PRIMERS OF MUSICAL BIOGRAPHY is to convey, as clearly as the limits of an elementary work will allow, a just idea of each composer's personality, and to record the principal events of his life. Knowledge of what a man is helps the understanding of what he does. These little books may serve, therefore, as a first step towards acquaintance with the genius and compositions of the masters to whom they are devoted."

# LUIGI CHERUBINI.

THE stranger in beautiful Florence cannot long remain oblivious of Cherubini. If he wander towards the south of the town, and stroll in the neighbourhood of the Barriera del Ponte Rosso, he will probably find himself in the Via Cherubini. If, in the course of sight-seeing, he visit the church of Sante Croce, his attention will surely be caught by a large and handsome monument bearing Cherubini's name; while, should his rambles take in a little street called Via Fiesolana, not far from the Piazza d'Azeglio, his curious eyes may light upon a tablet affixed to No. 22, and having an inscription thus translatable :—

Here was born on the xiv. September, MDCCLX., LUIGI CHERUBINI, who, famous in the science of Harmony, creator of sublime religious melodies, reformed every kind of musical style, and in the regions of art preserved intact among foreigners the glory of Italian supremacy.

A hundred and twenty-three years ago, that house—then numbered 6886, according to the now discarded custom of numbering by districts instead of streets—had as tenants a Signor Bartolomeo Cherubini, his wife, Verdiani (*née* Bosi), and their nine children. The bread-winner of the family followed the profession of music, not so as to attract men's eyes, but in a humble, if responsible, capacity as pianoforte accompanist (*maestro al cembalo*) at the Pergola Theatre. Bartolomeo was accounted a good musician, learned in all the learning of the schools, and having the scientific resources of the art at his fingers' ends. Picchianti, Cherubini's earliest biographer, himself a Florentine of the

B

period, describes the Pergola professor as "a chapelmaster strongly attached to the old customs of the art, and a rigid observer of the ancient scholastic discipline in his teaching." These words enable us to form a pretty accurate idea of Bartolomeo Cherubini. He would now be called a pedant, a "fifth-hunter," a slave to the "tone-families," and what not else that characterises a man who prefers the old ways to the new. We shall have very little more to say about him here, but it is important to observe what manner of musician he was, since his conservative instincts naturally influenced the training of those committed to his care. Bartolomeo seems to have been a good citizen and an exemplary husband and father. In his domestic capacity he doubtless rejoiced at the frequent additions to his house-hold. Verdiani, his wife, was only thirty-five years old when she presented him with a tenth child, and two others were subsequently born, so that the respectable Florentine professor fully attained the condition of blessedness described by the sacred writer who tells us that "Like as arrows in the hand of a giant even so are the young children." But though the family was prolific, it could hardly have been healthy. Of the twelve sons and daughters, only the tenth child lived to be old, and he, strange to say, was born into the world such a puny thing that his parents often looked with sadness into each other's faces when talk ran upon the babe's chances of life. The weak reed, however, survives the storm which hurls down the sturdy oak, and Bartolomeo Cherubini's tenth infant escaped all the perils and dangers that hung about its cradle.

The child's extreme fragility, let us here say, had some-thing to do with complicating a question that arose in after time as to the precise date of birth. A note introductory to the catalogue of Cherubini's works, and dictated by the master himself, fixes September 8, 1760, as the day when he came into the world. On the other hand, two certificates founded on the baptismal register are in existence, and agree in naming September 14. The authority of these attesta-tions is now accepted, and was acknowledged by Cherubini himself. We lean, however, to the doubt frankly expressed by M. Arthur Pougin, who says:—

It is true that Picchianti and M. Gamucci have each published an attestation derived from the baptismal registers of Santa Maria del Fiore; but this double attestation, while giving

September 15 as the date of the baptism—about which there cannot be any doubt—appears to fix on the 14th as the date of birth only by natural induction, and the general custom which requires children to be baptised on the day they are born, or the day after. Now the tradition so clearly set afloat by Cherubini himself, and preserved by him in the notice dictated to De Brauchesne, can hardly have sprung up spontaneously in his mind; it must have been based on family report—on the assertion of his father, or something of the kind—and I cannot help asking myself why and how it was that Cherubini subsequently abandoned it.

We submit that these are reasonable words, although Cherubini, after for many years keeping his birthday on the 8th, changed to the 14th, in deference to the authority of the baptismal register. There must have been some foundation for the belief in which the master remained as late as 1831, and those who accounted for the interval between the asserted date of birth (8th) and the actual date of baptism (14th) by reference to the child's extreme delicacy were, perhaps, not far wrong. As for the baptismal register, we are not disposed to give it great weight in the matter of birth. A hundred years ago, records of this kind were perfunctorily made, and for an indifferent official to assume that the baptised child had been born the day previous was perfectly natural and to be expected.

Concerning the early childhood of Cherubini little or nothing is known, for the reason, it may be, that there is little to tell. The boy no doubt found full scope for his energies in the act of living. We have his own authority for believing that at the age of six he began to study music under his father, so continuing till he was nine. Picchianti tells us what sort of progress was made by the little lad in studies which must have been of the driest character :—

Three years were enough for young Cherubini to obtain a sufficient knowledge of solfeggio, and of figured bass accompaniment and the tablature of the harpsichord, as they then called theoretical acquaintance with the keyboard, together with the art of placing the hands, and of the mechanism adapted for playing the instrument. He achieved this result before completing his ninth year, and without, on that account, neglecting the higher study of figures or languages.

The poor little boy must have worked hard to do this, for creative genius, though it may supply enthusiasm for study, does not necessarily mean capacity for the accumulation of facts, the retention of rules, and the mastering of problems which demand intellectual perception. Yet we see in the spectacle of a mere baby labouring at the unsympathetic elements of musical knowledge, striking proof of the very serious light in which the art was then regarded. Those days were not as ours in the matter of educating musicians by wholesale and with despatch, nor did pupils then consider themselves equipped for their career as soon as a few elementary rules had been mastered. Which will prove the better days, by reason of having a " more excellent way," we know full well, and the time may yet come when musical education will return to the hard plodding, the long-continued and thankless toil that gave us the great masters.

Bartolomeo Cherubini, at the end of the three years, placed his son under Bartolomeo Felici for the study of counterpoint and composition. This must have been about 1770, when, according to Fétis, Felici opened a musical academy in Florence, assisted by his son, Allessandro. Both professors were men of ability and distinction. Picchianti styles Alessandro a " remarkable artist," but enters more into detail concerning his father. Of him we read :—

Bartolomeo Felici, a man deeply versed in the musical science of his day, was a profound and skilful contrapuntist. The compositions in the *alla capella* style of his which have been handed down to us are models of purity, clearness and ingenious artifice — qualities causing them to be heard with pleasure whenever they are now sung in our churches. For teaching the difficult art of composition he was reputed the best professor in Florence and all Tuscany, and his school was attended by a large number of pupils, whose productions subsequently sustained his credit and glory.

In the hands of such a man young Cherubini was safe, although there is reason to believe that Felici taught according to the cumbrous, embarrassing and unscientific method then prevalent in Italian schools. We read in Picchianti :—

Despite the impetus given in the opening years of the century to the new theory of music by the celebrated Rameau, and subsequently by various illustrious Italians, the theory still remained enveloped in the physical phenomena of sound, and continued to be based upon calculations and geometrical demonstrations referring only to the mathematical determination of the number of vibrations—that is, of the volume or other elements of the sonorous body—whence it resulted that such and such intervals were admissible in musical compositions. . . . Theory being in this state, and absolutely unable to offer clear and sufficiently developed rules for the study of harmony and modulation, blind practice was substituted for it. The consequence of all this was that the art of counterpoint was encumbered with a host of observations and rules, each of which, invariably deduced from particular cases and not from general principles, gave rise to a host of exceptions. To succeed in mastering all the rules and the aggregate of all the exceptions, the student was obliged to go through a long and fatiguing process ; he had to compose examples of counterpoint, first simple and then with certain artifices, both above and below a melody in plain song, the master making him write a single part and then combine in various manners six, seven, and eight real parts, with all scholastic and pedantic rigour.

Unscientific as this system may have been, we know that marvels of contrapuntal skill came out of it. It severely tried patience and perseverance, and possibly disgusted with music many who, travelling along a less thorny road, would have gone on to the end. Those who endured the test were of the right stuff. They certainly knew how to use the technical resources of their art, and there was reason to believe that something more than a capacity for plodding had carried them through.

Cherubini remained with Felici four years, but began composing before he quitted that master's school. Boy-like, he aimed at a high mark, and produced a Mass for chorus and orchestra. Of this work nothing is known, save that it was performed (1773) in one of the Florentine churches. Other pieces followed in quick succession, as the master himself has told us :—

Cherubini composed successively, from 1773 to 1778, seventeen pieces, comprising masses, interludes, psalms, oratorios, and separate airs, all performed with equal success in the churches and amateur theatres of his native town.

The autograph catalogue gives us some particulars concerning these boyish works. They included two masses, besides the one already mentioned, both in C major, a Cantata, "La Publica Felicità," in honour of the Grand Duke, a "Magnificat," two "Lamentations of Jeremiah," a "Miserere," a comic air, and a "Te Deum." The fact that all the lad's compositions of this period were heard publicly shows that they were held in esteem. Yet it does not appear that a special genius shone through them as it did through those of Mozart and Mendelssohn. To this Halévy speaks in his "*Etudes sur la Vie et les Travaux de Cherubini.*" As the master's favourite pupil and friend, Halévy was permitted to examine the musical papers which Cherubini, who jealously guarded them from prying eyes, left behind him. He says:—

I saw, on going through them, that it was, as it were, out of respect for himself, and from a desire to spare these early works, that he had kept them from all eyes. Everything in them announced the intelligent child brought up in a good school, and nurtured on good precepts; but nothing indicated the genius which was destined to be revealed at a later period. The Cherubini who had become illustrious was anxious about his reputation as a child, and fearful of injuring the glory of the Cherubini of thirteen. It was a sort of not unbecoming and pardonable coquetry.

Let no one suppose that Cherubini from the time of leaving Felici gave himself up entirely to composition. He had worked hard—even to drudgery, we may well believe—for seven years, but his studies, so thorough and comprehensive, were only half completed. Therefore he put himself under Pietro Bizarri for singing, and Giuseppe Castrucci for the organ and piano, remaining with them till he had attained his seventeenth year. By that time Cherubini was, in some sort, a notability in Florence. The citizens, jealous for the artistic repute of their famous town, accounted him a prodigy, and cherished the highest hopes of his future. All this, of course, delighted the family in the Via Fiesolana, but it failed to remove the difficulty that confronted them, and found expression in the query, "What is next to be done with our Luigi Carlo Zanobia Salvadore Maria?" The youth was pluming his wings for flight. He longed to see men and cities, to enlarge the field of his observation, and vary the nature of his experience. In these respects, his father, now the happy parent of a dozen children, could not help him. The swarm of young mouths open for daily bread consumed all the poor professor's earnings, and it seemed for the moment that Number Ten's career would be checked for want of a little money. Happily, the Grand Ducal Throne was then occupied by a prince in whom survived the spirit of Lorenzo the Magnificent. Leopold, afterwards the Austrian Emperor of that name, knew his duty to such a city as Florence, and lost no opportunity of promoting its material prosperity or artistic renown. When, therefore, it came to his ears that a lad in the Via Fiesolana had the spirit of music upon him, he took a real interest in the case. Leopold did not stop at a smile and a compliment—very flattering royal gifts, no doubt, but often barren. He put his hand in his pocket—took up the quality of father at the point where Bartolomeo's slender purse obliged him to stop—and made young Cherubini an allowance sufficient to pay the cost of study under the famous Sarti, then resident at Bologna. The opening of the year 1778, the youth being then nearly eighteen, witnessed this real and royal start in life.

Sarti's influence upon Cherubini was destined in the nature of things to be great, since the young Florentine entered his school with all the ardent worship that youth gives to its ideal. It need hardly be said that reverence and devotion were not wasted upon such a man. Sarti was a musician to whom all the world accorded high rank. " His compositions," says Miel, one of Cherubini's biographers, " were characterised as divine; every town in Italy wanted him to write something for it, and he was unable to satisfy the demands made on him from all quarters." Outside his native land, he secured the admiration of connoisseurs such as Joseph Haydn, " Sarti being one of the masters," writes Frammery, " whom he esteemed most highly, no doubt because the Italian's energetic and noble style possessed a greater analogy than that of any other composer to his own." At the time when Cherubini went to him he was fifty years of age, and in the zenith of his powers. The lad soon found himself in an atmosphere very different from that he had quitted. It was not so much that Sarti made him study Palestrina, and write anthems in the style of that great master. Cherubini might have expected this, knowing Sarti's preference for Palestrina. What he did not antici-pate, perhaps, was passing from unmixed scholasticism to something of the ideal and romantic. Certain authorities tell us that the Bolognese teacher directed his pupils to " imitate him in composing at night in a large unfurnished room, with a lamp suspended from the ceiling, that shed only a glimmering light." Such an attempt to excite the imagination by the influence of outward conditions is common enough in our day, but must have been surprising at the height of the "powder and pigtail" era. Sarti is said also to have made his pupils copy the scores of the masters in great quantities. But he did a more practical thing in the case of Cherubini. Sarti, as we have seen, was a very busy man, and had more work on his hands than one pair could get through. Consequently, knowing the quality of the young Florentine, he intrusted him with the padding of his numerous operas. The step was safe, as well as convenient, because an Italian public at that time had no ears for the minor characters in a lyric drama. They listened to a few leading airs and concerted pieces; as the rest went on they talked. None the less were Cherubini's labours a valuable exercise and an important experience; obtained, moreover, without personal responsibility or risk, since, had his music been bad, and anybody paid attention to it, censure would have fallen upon Sarti, as the supposed author.

In 1779 a vacancy occured in the musical staff of Milan Cathedral through the death of the chapelmaster, Signor Fioroni, and Sarti having been chosen to fill it, removed from Bologna to the northern city, taking Cherubini with him. By that time the master had conceived a strong affection for the pupil, who himself tells us in the autograph note already mentioned, that Sarti gave him excellent advice, and made him his travelling companion on artistic journeys. Naturally, therefore, an opportunity was soon found for the young man to produce an opera on his own account. This he did a year after the removal to Milan, when a work in three acts, "Il Quinto Fabio," was brought out at Alexandria. Nothing is known of the opera now, but a tradition exists that it had no particular success, and we know that the composer did not preserve the score. From the date of " Il quinto Fabio " till September, 1781, Cherubini was several times away from Milan, engaged in the task of directing other operas. Thus, in 1781, he went to Venice, where rehearsal, owing to the bankruptcy of the manager, did not ripen into performance. In January, 1782, he produced " Armida " (three acts) at the Pergola, Florence; " Adriano in Sirio " (three acts) followed at Leghorn in May; and four months later he was again at Florence with another three-act work, entitled " Messenzio." Besides these things, he wrote during the same period a Motett for the singer Marchesi; a second Motett for two choirs and two organs, "Nemo gaudeat"; and a number of smaller pieces; to which we allude only for the purpose of showing his remarkable assiduity. It may be added that two of the pieces in question were duets, with accompaniments for two corni d'amour—a now obsolete instrument, of which the English nobleman (Lord Cowper) who ordered the works was an amateur.

Another biographer (Arnold), quoted by Mr. Bellasis, declares that Cherubini's operatic music proved too learned for the taste of his countrymen: "People were afraid of him, for the evidence of originality displayed in his compositions might do considerable harm to their beloved cantilenas and fioriture." But this did not interfere with his progress, though it might have encouraged him to believe that he had done his work in the schools, and needed the experience of active life beyond their narrow limits. He left Sarti in the autumn of 1782, and began his career in earnest.

During the following year, our young master brought out two operas—one, "Il Quinto Fabio" (No. 2), at the Teatro Argentina, Rome; the other, "La Sposo di Tre," at the San Samuele, Venice. The last was a two-act *opera buffo*, and both are now extinct. Both, however, served the purpose of making their young composer better known and liked. After hearing the comic work, the Venetians called him "Il Cherubino," because of the sweetness of his melodies, according to some, but, if we may credit M. Félix Clément, on account of his handsome face and figure. As M. Clément is generally wrong on disputed points, we prefer to believe that Cherubini's themes and not his bodily graces caused the pretty play upon his name. On leaving Venice, where he had made so favourable an impression, "Il Cherubino" proceeded to Florence and saw his native city for the last time; remaining there long enough to direct the performance of a *pasticcio* oratorio at the Jesuits' Church, the music being all taken and adapted from his own operas save, perhaps, one number expressly written. Cherubini also produced at Florence during this visit an opera entitled "L'Idalide," shortly following that work up with "L'Alessandro nell' Indie" at Mantua. By this time, although Cherubini was only in his twenty-fourth year, his name was known far and wide, even in the distant island whence came his early patron, Lord Cowper. There he was admired to some practical purpose ; since, soon after the Mantuan engagement, he received an offer to go to London for the purpose of writing two Italian operas and producing them at the King's Theatre in 1785-6. Picchianti tells us that the directorship of a Philharmonic Society then existing in London was included in this transaction, but M. Pougin questions the statement on what appear to be good grounds. In the first place, Cherubini makes no mention of the matter in his autobiographical note ; in the second place, the catalogue contains no mention of works written for the Society named. On the other hand, M. Pougin believes, with Choron and Fazelle, that the young master received here the title and duties of Composer to the King, and wrote several detached pieces in discharge of his functions.

Cherubini left Florence for England in September, 1784, two months after the Handel Commemoration in Westminster Abbey, and thus not only severed his connection with Italy, but entered upon a course which led to his complete departure from the accepted Italian style.

There is trustworthy evidence to the effect that Cherubini made no very considerable figure in London. For example, little is said about him in the English musical history of the period. Lord Mount Edgcumbe does not even mention the composer's name under this date in his well-known "Reminiscences," and Parkes, the oboist, whose chatty "Memoirs" are full of personal observations, dismisses him in a few lines. We read in the last-named work :—

The Italian opera was this year (1786) acted by Signor Babini and Signora Sestini. They appeared in a new opera of Paesiello, entitled " Il Marchese Tulipano," under the direction of Cherubini.

There is also a reference to the production of our master's pasticcio opera, " Demetrio," in the course of which it is said :—

Cherubini, who selected and composed this opera, was a scholar of Sarti ; he was a young man of genius, and the overture and the duet in the third act gave promise of future greatness.

Beyond these meagre words, written at a time when Cherubini had achieved the greatness promised in 1786, the gossiping Parkes has nothing to say. Dr. Burney is hardly more communicative. He styles Cherubini the " nominal composer" to the King, and devotes but very few lines to the young Italian's work in London. The whole subject, indeed, is barren, for even Mr. Bellasis, who cannot be charged with wanting a spirit of research, fills scarcely more than a page with Cherubini's doings. Fétis dismisses the same theme in a dozen lines, while the author of the article " Cherubini," in Grove's " Dictionary of Music and Musicians" makes nine lines suffice. Certain facts stand out, however, with sufficient clearness. One is that Cherubini made as favourable an impression as could be looked for in the case of a young and almost unknown man. It is certain, likewise, that he was well received in the highest society. The master himself remarks in his short autobiography :—

During his stay in London he had the honour of being presented to the Prince of Wales, afterwards Regent, and then King under the name of George IV. This prince was very fond of music, especially vocal music. Cherubini played on several occasions with him and the Duke of Quisbourg (Queensbury ?), with whom he was very well acquainted.

The actual amount of work done in London by Cherubini we shall perhaps never know. No two writers bear precisely the same evidence, but it appears that beside " Demetrio," for which six numbers were written, he produced a comic opera, " La Finta Principessa," and one of serious import, "Giulio Sabini," libretto by Metastasio. This last was, according to Burney, killed by an inefficient representation, much to the chagrin of the composer.

At the close of the season of 1785 Cherubini went to Paris—a mere holiday trip, but one big with fate, as such things often are in a world where the unexpected always happens. In the autobiography we read :—

Towards the end of July this year he paid a visit to Paris, where he first made the acquaintance of the celebrated Viotti, with whom he formed a close friendship and with whom he promised to come and spend the next year in that capital. It was during this visit that he was presented to Marie Antoinette, by whom he was most favourably received, and who expressed a wish to hear some of his music at the concerts which took place in the Château of Versailles.

Cherubini owed what he had of royal favour at this time to the good offices of Viotti, who took the greatest interest in his gifted countryman, and laid himself out to serve him. On this matter M. Pougin says :—

Having amassed a veritable fortune on his grand European tour, he was in consequence independent, and divided the pleasant and smiling existence he led in Paris between important labours in composition, the care he bestowed on his pupils, numerous mundane relations and periods of intelligent and studious leisure. When Cherubini, preceded by the great reputation he had achieved in his own country, came, to a certain extent accidentally, and made his first stay in Paris, Viotti, whose generous sentiments were equal to his admirable artistic powers, determined to know him, and welcomed him like a brother. Older by some years, already settled a considerable time in the French capital, where he possessed an immense circle of acquaintances, and well versed in the artistic life of the day, Viotti constituted himself in some sort the protector, the guide, and the mentor of his compatriot, infusing into his intercourse with the latter such amenity, graciousness, and affectionate cordiality that Cherubini, touched by such conduct, soon returned sentiment for sentiment, and an almost fraternal intimacy, never afterwards to be disturbed, was thenceforth established between them.

Nothing could have been more fortunate for the Italian stranger than Viotti's sympathy and support. It meant friendship in a strange land, and more, it meant professional help. Not only did Cherubini obtain through Viotti a royal audience, but by the same means, as Pougin suspects, and we are ready to believe, he gained a hearing at the Sacred Concerts, then under the direction of Legros, once an operatic singer. At those entertainments Cherubini made his first public appearance in Paris (September 8, 1785), when a "symphony" and three airs from his pen were performed. The "symphony" was doubtless an overture, the master never having written a work of the class now specifically so called. It is of course impossible to ascertain the precise reception accorded to the master and his music, but at least one of the critics was hard upon both. Searching the files of the *Mercure de France*—a print very well known in connection with the Gluck-Picinni squabble—M. Pougin came on the following :—

At the concert on the 8th inst. we heard several airs by a new Italian composer, M. Cherubini. They were a symphony and three airs. The symphony must have confirmed the opinion of those who consider that this style of writing is not that in which Italian composers distinguish themselves. The airs appeared to possess greater merit; the incoherence of the ideas and the small amount of character and interest in the motives, however, were indicative of the composer's youth.

However mortified by opinions like the foregoing, Cherubini felt that his trip to Paris had borne good fruit. Thanks to Viotti, he could number amongst his acquaintances such people as Mesdames de Polignac and de Richelieu, MM. Florian, Marmontel, and Abbé Marellet; and he obtained a footing in the famous "Société Academique des Enfans d'Apollon," at one of whose concerts he first heard a symphony by Haydn, and "learned," says Arnold, in a passage every word of which we endorse, "how to combine depth with lightness, grace with power, jest with earnestness, toying with dignity."

Cherubini returned to England for the opera season of 1787, but soon after the failure of "Giulio Sabini" he quitted our country and kept a promise to Viotti, by going to reside permanently with him in Paris. It must not be supposed that he retired from London in dudgeon. The opera was "strangled at its very birth," as Burney expresses it, through no fault in itself; wherefore Cherubini, though greatly vexed, discharged his duties conscientiously to the end of the season, and also had printed and published in London a set of six nocturnes.

The circumstances attendant upon our master's return to Paris may be gathered from his autobiography, in which we read :—

He was again presented to Queen Marie Antoinette, who received him with as much kindness as ever, and admitted him to the private concerts she gave in the Château de Versailles, at the Princess de Polignac's, where she sang, and where pieces of Cherubini's, rendered by the celebrated Garat, were among the compositions performed. At this period, too, Viotti urged him to undertake a French opera, and for this purpose made him acquainted with Marmontel, who intrusted him with the book of "Démophon," which he began to set.

The master's next effort, however, was destined to be made in the land of his birth and in the capital of the Sardinian kingdom. For fifteen months he remained in Paris, doing nothing of which trace is left, except write a cantata, "Amphion," for the Olympic Lodge, and set music to eighteen romances from Florian's "Estelle." That otherwise he was not, strictly speaking, idle, may be assumed in the case of a man who left behind him so many proofs of industry. Perhaps he devoted himself to the study and meditation which must, at some time or other have preceded the remarkable development his genius soon after underwent. But, however this may be, we know that he made good his footing within the charmed circle of Parisian artistic and social life. Miel states, in his "Notice Historique sur J. B. Viotti," that he assisted at the *matinées* given every Sunday by the great violinist in the apartments common to them both, while his favourite pupil, Halévy, tells us, in the interesting "Etudes sur la vie et les travaux de Cherubini":—

People's saloons were thrown open to him, and he was admitted to all the sweet delights of high Parisian life. . . . It was a happy time for him, because he felt greatly flattered at this success. He was then eight-and-twenty. A portrait, painted somewhere about this time by Mdlle. Dumont and preserved in his family, represents him as elegant, neat, endowed with a noble and expressive physiognomy and a persuasive look. The world liked him and he liked the world. He was for a moment the fashion, and became a "lion." He used to speak with pleasure of this period of his life, and retained an agreeable recollection of all the delicate marks of respect and all the little attentions then paid him.  ·

It is, perhaps, hardly to be wondered at that the master sat at his desk very seldom under conditions so fascinating to a still youthful man.

The time came, however, when he had to fulfil an engagement made in 1784 to write an opera for the Turin season of 1787-8. To this end all the dear delights of Paris were given up, and in October Cherubini set out for the Sardinian capital, where he wrote his "Ifigenia in Aulide," and produced it during the month of February following. The new opera was received in a manner extremely gratifying, despite the fact that it paid scant heed to the traditions of the Italian stage. *A propos* M. Pougin has discovered, in the *Calendrier Musical* for 1789, a letter addressed to the editors, in which some interesting details of this event are given. Subjoined is an extract therefrom :—

At a moment when admirers of the lyric stage are regretting Gluck and Sacchini, it is consoling to announce another artist, who, though still very young, is even now producing the fruit of the ripest talent. This artist, already known by several successes in Italy, is M. Cherubini. He has just brought out at Turin an "Ifigenia in Aulide," which owes its extraordinarily flattering reception principally to the composer's efforts thoroughly to ally the musical effect to the sense of the words, a plan almost unknown in Italy, and interesting for our stage, to which M. Cherubini intends to devote himself. The music of the new "Iphigenia," is, so they write from Italy, in a style quite new to this country; now sublime, now tender, but invariably energetic and attractive, it produced almost unheard-of effects. The Court even could not resist the general enthusiasm. Our princes, who do not usually applaud performances, applauded a great deal, such is the power of superior merit to extort imperiously tributes of praise.

It is curious to read here of a movement towards greater dramatic truth, when the present struggle, fought on the same ground, appears to indicate that it has only just begun. But between the reforms set on foot by Cherubini a hundred years ago and those now advocated in the name of progress, there is a difference indeed. It may be interesting to cite the opinion of Halévy with regard to the work in which Cherubini made his first step on an independent course. The French composer says in the "Etude" already spoken of:—

This opera differs in style from Cherubini's preceding operas. It is already more nervous. We see springing up in it a certain freshness and vitality of which Italian musicians of his time were ignorant, or for which they did not care. It was the dawn of a new day; Cherubini was preparing for the struggle. Gluck had accustomed France to the sublime energy of his masterpieces; Mozart had just written in Germany "Le Nozze di Figaro" and "Don Giovanni." It would not do to be left behind; it would not do to be beaten; in the lists he was about to enter he would meet two giants. Like an athlete before descending into the arena, he anointed his limbs; like a warrior about to engage in combat, he girded up his loins.

The struggle, however, was not to take place on the Italian stage, but in the great arena which witnessed Gluck's triumphs. With "Ifigenia in Aulide" Cherubini took leave of his native country. He wrote no more Italian operas, and when he crossed the Italian frontier on his way back to Paris he bade "the land of song" a final farewell. Thenceforth he was a Frenchman. Halévy, from whose rhetoric we have just quoted, credits Cherubini with a presentiment of eternal separation from his native country, and fancies that the well-known trio in "Ifigenia" is the expression of a natural sorrow.   He remarks :—

Perhaps in this noble and sweet piece of inspiration he was addressing a last farewell to his country, which he was about to leave, and leave for ever, since, despite the desire and wish I have frequently heard him express, it was never his lot to see Italy again.   Perhaps he felt remorse on the eve of adopting another land as his own.   At the moment of consummating a voluntary exile, and of abandoning the country of his birth, perhaps a secret instinct, one of those voices that never deceive, warned him that the separation would be eternal ; that he would not behold Florence, or the beloved family he left there, any more.   A mournful reminiscence must have been awakened in his heart.   It seems as though the beautiful trio, which it is impossible to hear without emotion, was the echo of this profound regret.

The foregoing is no doubt pretty sentiment and may have a basis of fact.   On the other hand, it is very likely that Cherubini anticipated the future as little as any of us, and had no more idea of saying to Italy "Good-bye for ever" than had Robinson Crusoe of a prolonged absence from England when he dropped down the river on his memorable voyage.

Serious work awaited Cherubini in Paris, whither he returned in March, 1788, only a few days after the production of "Ifigenia."   Some time previous, the Opéra had accepted a lyric drama from Vogel—at that time a popular composer— on the subject of Démophon.  The book, according to Pougin— Fétis tells quite a different story, which need not be credited —was written by Desriaux, and the artistic world generally believed that Vogel had finished his part of the task before death overtook him.   It is certain, at any rate, that the overture was several times performed in public with brilliant success.   Naturally the public looked for the work, and were somewhat annoyed when it appeared that Marmontel and Cherubini were engaged upon the same subject, with every prospect of having their labours preferred to those of Desriaux and the departed Vogel.   A fatal prejudice very nearly arose on this score, nor were matters improved by the fact that Marmontel, a hot partisan of Picinni in the late war, had many opponents only too ready to serve him an evil turn.

However, Cherubini's "Démophon" went over the head of Vogel's, and was produced September 5, 1788. As to the effect it made, contemporary evidence is not altogether of one mind; still, reading between the lines in certain cases, it is possible to get at the facts. The *Mercure de France*, a friendly witness, declared in a first notice :—

"Démophon" was very successful from beginning to end. In our next number we will go more into details concerning the very numerous beauties to be found in the poem and in the music.

Later, the same journal remarked :—

The score has now been judged by its true value, and the composer has reason to feel satisfied with the opinion thus formed—namely, that it was impossible for any one so young and with such a slight knowledge of our stage to begin more brilliantly, and that the work proves he possesses everything requisite to do still better.

Then came a number of qualifying criticisms, put with the skill of a practised journalist when he desires to justify his own perspicacity without hurting a composer's feelings. These we need not quote, one fact being more eloquent than many words—the fact that "Démophon" was performed only eight times and then withdrawn.

Fétis, who is more trustworthy as a critic than historian, takes pains to set forth the reasons why "Démophon" so soon broke down, and lays much stress upon Cherubini's sudden plunge into the difficulties of a new stage and a strange language. He writes :—

The score furnishes a curious subject of historical study, if compared with "Ifigenia," which Cherubini wrote in Turin at the beginning of the same year. In the latter score melody abounds, and, among several numbers full of charm, we remark a trio of the greatest beauty. "Démophon," on the contrary, offers us only aridity in the cantilenas, vague motives, numerous defects in the rhythm and symmetry of the phrases, and, what is worse than all, languishing monotony in the general colour of the work. Even the harmony has nothing distinguished about it, and it is difficult to recognise in this feeble production the hand of a man who soon afterwards justly caused himself to be considered a great master. Whence could arise the embarrassment which thus oppressed his genius?

Fétis answers this question by reference to the novelty of the composer's position, and also by indicating the character

C

of Marmontel's " pretended and detestable lyric verses."
He says:—

Poor Cherubini did not know what to do with these verses ot
all sizes, which sometimes compelled him to make his phrase
five bars, and sometimes allowed him only two, or forced him
to augment the value of the musical *tempi*, so as to make two
bars out of one.   The composition of this opera must have been
a long torture to him.

Let us add here the words of Halévy:—

I regret that Cherubini, on arriving in Paris, should have
fallen into the hands of Morellet and Marmontel. . . . That had
occurred to Cherubini which happens to a traveller who, thrown
into the heart of a great city with which he is not acquainted, asks
his way from great lords and the like—men only accustomed
to go out in carriages.   With the best faith in the world, they
give him false directions and lead him astray.   An honest
*bourgeois* who plods the streets on foot would be worth a hundred
times as much.

On this matter of Marmontel's work we have no desire to
challenge the evidence; but, bad as his verses may have
been, they did not alone bring about failure.   No opera with
really good music in it was ever ruined by a poor libretto.
The power of the composer, armed with all the potent
means of an irresistible art, conceals the weakness of the
poet; and in the case of " Démophon " we are bound to
conclude that Cherubini had not familiarised himself with
the highly dramatic French school into which he abruptly
passed from the pure melodiousness of Italy.   According to
some eminent critics the change, though abrupt, was not
complete enough for success, Cherubini taking into his new
style not a few traditions from the old, and thus producing a
composite work adapted to please neither Italians on the
one hand nor French on the other.   M. Pougin is of this
opinion, and writes:—

. . . despite himself the old Adam sometimes reappeared, and
was seen sacrificing, almost without suspecting it, to the gods
of his early years.   Hence certain discrepancies and an inevitable
inequality in the entirety, as such, of his work, which appeared
somewhat composite, and in which, on account of too great an
amount of reflection, the inspiration lacked abundance and
spontaniety.

Years ago, in his work on the Académie Impériale de Musique, Castil-Blaze expressed the same idea :—

" Démophon " marks the epoch when the musician changed his style. The author has not yet any settled system ; the beginner navigates his bark between Gluck and Picinni. His airs, graceful and tender in expression, belong to the Italian manner, which he abandons directly a strong situation arises."

The failure of " Démophon " seems to have invested Cherubini's position in Paris with a measure of uncertainty. It was more than an artistic rebuff, since it entailed pecuniary loss. The master himself bears witness to this in an autographic note written late in life :—

I first supported myself (at Paris) on what I earned at London, but that was not much, and then on the trifle for which I agreed to write an opera in 1787 at Turin. On coming back to Viotti's in Paris I composed " Démophon," which was played at the Grand Opéra in December (?), 1788. This work gave me author's rights, but they did not bring in much, seeing that it was performed only eight times, and that even the little I made was swallowed up by what I had to expend for having unluckily taken it into my head to have the opera engraved at my own cost.

His impecunious circumstances were not much relieved, we may suppose, by the writing of a cantata, " Circé," for one of the Olympian Lodge concerts, though he may have felt honoured on hearing it sung by Rousseau. Happily light soon broke through the dark clouds and Cherubini found place and pay.

The circumstances attendant upon this change in Cherubini's position are fully set forth by M. Pougin, according to whom there were in Paris, just before the Revolution broke out, only nine real theatres open to the public, and three of these—the Opéra, the Comédie-Française, and the Comédie-Italienne—were almost reserved for aristocratic, artistic and literary society. The time was fully ripe for enterprise in drama, and, as usual, with the hour came the man, who, strangely enough, stepped out of Marie Antoinette's tiring-room, in the person of her hairdresser, Léonard. This individual had a soul above the curling-tongs, and a vision that took in more than the pomade-pot. Seeing his opportunity, and justly measuring the advantage given him by nearness to the royal ear, he availed himself of both so well

that a patent from Louis XVI. soon empowered him to open
a new theatre in Paris, devoted equally to Italian opera,
French opera, and comedy, and to be called the "Théâtre
de Monsieur," after the distinctive title of the Count de
Provence, his Majesty's brother. Léonard lost no time in
forming a partnership with Viotti, who knew better than a
hairdresser what to do with a theatre, and who had such
confidence in the venture that he risked upon it all his
fortune. Others being confident, likewise, a joint-stock
company was formed, a lease of the theatre in the Tuileries
—where "Monsieur" dwelt—obtained for thirty years, and
a company of artists got together by Viotti himself, who
brought from Italy what has been called "the most admirable
troupe that had ever appeared in France." Few operatic
enterprises ever started so well. M. Pougin gives the names
of the chief performers, and a magnificent list it is; while in
the roll-call of the band we see Rode, Baillot, Hugo,
Duvernoy, Schmerza, Othon, and others scarcely less
famous. As a matter of course, Viotti found a post for
his dear friend Cherubini, who, we are told, was "intrusted
with the highest direction of musical matters, as well as
with the mission of watching over the studies of the artists;
of undertaking the modifications it might be deemed useful
to make in the Italian works produced; and lastly, of
composing the new numbers thought necessary to be inter-
polated." The enterprise in which our master was thus
honourably employed launched itself before the world on
January 26, 1789, when Tritta's opera, " Le Vicende
Amorosa " was performed.

Cherubini's position at the Théâtre de Monsieur, though
decidedly honourable, was not very remunerative. His
annual salary did not exceed 4,000 francs, for which he
engaged to superintend rehearsals and act as composer to
the house, writing two French operas every year, and having,
according to the then custom, no property in them. It is
true that he was rarely required to fulfil the conditions, and
between 1789 and 1794 produced only two operas; but on
the other hand, he had to labour hard upon the works
played by the Italian section of the company. MM. Viotti
and Léonard were wise enough to know that Italian opera
*pur et simple* would never do for the French, who required
more dramatic interest and truth than satisfied Cherubini's
countrymen. Hence they kept a poet on the premises to

alter libretti; Cherubini's business being to provide music wherever the changes made required it. As the management was unusually active, producing twenty French and Italian operas in eleven months, this involved a good deal of toil. Cherubini, however, felt quite content. He occupied a post which kept him before the public, and enabled him rapidly to build up a reputation.

The new venture fell upon troublous times. In the first place, Viotti and Léonard could not open on the date announced, because of, as official advertisements put it, the "extreme rigour of the cold." Next, the house had to be closed for the Easter holidays; next, the performances were interrupted by the taking of the Bastile and attendant events; lastly, the theatre had to be given up because, after the abortive flight to Varennes, the royal family were brought to Paris and lodged in the Tuileries, under the same roof. This event happened, as every reader of history knows, in October, 1789, but the company did not give their last performance at the Théâtre de Monsieur till December 23. On closing the doors they were literally homeless, and advertised as follows: "To-day and to-morrow there will be no performance. The public will be informed by fresh bills when and where the performances will be continued." We may assume that no one concerned measured the significance of political circumstances at this moment. The abyss of the Revolution did not yet yawn in the nation's path, and men hoped and believed that king and people would find a way of settling their differences. Undismayed, therefore, by the stormy aspect of things, Viotti engaged a building at the Foire St. Germain, and opened it as the Théâtre de Monsieur on January 10, 1790, the opera chosen for the occasion being Paisiello's "Il Barbiere," a work destined in after years to be extinguished by the "Barbiere" of Rossini. These quarters were, of course, but temporary, and in less than twelve months Viotti and Léonard had a new theatre ready, which they called the Théâtre Feydeau. The first performance at this house took place in January, 1791; and in the same year Cherubini produced his first French opera, "Lodoiska," breaking for ever with the Italian style he had theretofore cultivated, and entering upon a new path leading to highest honour and fortune. The fortunes of the new Théâtre Feydeau were soon darkened by shadows which the splendid success of "Lodoiska" could not disperse. Before the events of '92-3, all interests gave way. The Italian section of Viotti's company hurried out of France pell-mell, frightened by the terrible 10th of August. Léonard, compromised by some sort of connection with the flight to Varennes, also put the frontier between himself and the revolutionaries, and Viotti escaped to England. The French company were thus left without leaders, upon which, following the fashion of the day, they constituted a republic—in other words, a joint-stock company—and carried on the enterprise for a common profit.

Cherubini's work at the Théâtre Feydeau previous to the break-up just described will ever be memorable on account of the "new departure" he made in "Lodoiska." The master had, from the first days of Léonard and Viotti's enterprise, charmed French ears by his beautiful additions to the Italian operas performed. These gave him repute, and influenced in his favour the jury to whom he had resolved to submit a typical French work, which, while melodious with Italian tune, should be dramatic in its musical characterisation. "Lodoiska" at once became a town's talk, the newspapers especially going into raptures over it. "M. Cherubini's music," said the *Almanach Général de Tous la Spectacles,* "is comparable to nothing less than the sublimest efforts of the greatest masters. . . . Never did French ears listen to more expressive and characteristic music." *Les Spectacles de Paris* exclaimed: "A grandiose subject: a frightful conflagration and enchanting music!" The *Annales Dramatiques* declared:—

This music is entrancing—sublime; a broad style, admirable treatment of the masses, profound orchestration, astonishing dash, surprising originality, and grand touches—this is what it offers us, and which justifies the enthusiasm of the public, who during the performances rose at every piece and applauded the immortal author.

On its part, the weighty and influential *Journal de Paris* said:—

The style of the words is beneath mediocrity. Just the contrary must be stated of the music, which is that of a great master. The public were informed whose it was, and it was only natural for them to expect a very great deal from the young composer. Despite of this they were none the less astonished at the brilliant effects with which he has profusely adorned his work. . . . We scarcely know an instance of more vigorous and more fertile talent. We are compelled sometimes to think it is too much so; if there is anything we could wish in the music, it is a trifle more melody, which would enable the audience to rest after the exceedingly numerous orchestral effects.

Another critic, quoted by Mr. Bellasis, echoes this last remark, observing :—

If we have a reproach to utter about the music of this work, it is this—it is too beautiful; and this is a real reproach. All the pieces, worked out with infinite care, and all equally worked out, do not give the listener time to breathe ; by being forced to admire, you end by being fatigued with too-continued beauty; you would prefer from time to time simpler pieces on which to take repose.

What, let us ask in passing, would these writers have said to a Wagner opera with its orchestra in full blast the whole time, and scores of *Leitmotiven* calling for recognition and comprehension ? However, the too great beauty of " Lodoiska " did not stand in its way, the work being performed two hundred times in one year. If it be asked wherein the peculiar qualities of Cherubini's opera are found, we cannot do better than quote a writer in the *Neiderrrheinische Musik-Zeitung*, who says :—

While Cherubini carried out in the melody the fundamental law of dramatic truth, the agreement of the music with the situations in the drama, and their poetic expression as laid down by Gluck, he exhibited greater depth of intention, fuller and bolder harmony, and a style of instrumentation which, by its richness and the characteristic employment of the wind instruments, especially in conformity with the peculiar quality of their sound, introduced the orchestra in a brilliant manner, not only as the foundation for the vocal portion, but also as its necessary adjunct and its equal in bringing about the theatrical effect as a whole.

On the same subject M. Pougin remarks :—

By the new forms he adopted in his score of " Lodoiska," by the vigour displayed in its general conception, by the power he succeeded in giving to his orchestra, and by the truly architectural structure of this virile production of his genius, Cherubini came forward as the determined champion of the evolution which comic opera, that style of composition so eminently French, was about to go through. Dramatic truth, the study of grand situations, and the portrayal of character, which Gluck had so successfully introduced amongst us in lyric drama properly so called, were all things Cherubini determined to transport to the stage of the Théâtre Feydeau, and endow with them our musical comedy, which, with a few exceptions, had hardly been distinguished for delicacy or wit, grace or tenderness, and which was pretty generally deficient in breadth and emotion.

These extracts amply suffice to show wherein consisted the distinctive merit of " Lodoiska," and in what manner and degree Cherubini appeared as a reformer of opera.

Cherubini bent a little to the storm which drove his employers and many of his colleagues out of the country. In the delirium of the hour Paris was a dangerous place for people who had been in any way associated with the fallen *régime.* Our master, therefore, withdrew from the capital to a house at La Chartreuse de Gaillon, near Rouen, where lived his friend Louis, the architect. In the company of this gentleman and his wife, an accomplished musician, who had even written and produced, at the Favart, an opéra-comique, " Fleur d'Epine," Cherubini spent some months of '92, and nearly all the *année terrible,* '93. It was there he received news that his father had passed away, and there that, not being absorbed by dramatic composition, he wrote a number of his smaller works. " Koukourgi," an unfinished three-act opera, belongs to this date, as does, on the evidence of Cherubini's own biographical notes, a two-act opera entitled " Elise, ou le Mont Saint-Bernard."

The master returned to Paris towards the end of 1793, and soon events happened which had the greatest possible influence upon his future life. In the first place he married a lady with whom he had been for some time in love. Her name was Anne Cécile Tourette, and her station that of daughter in the family of an obscure music-teacher once attached to the Chapel Royal. Cherubini's marriage was not, therefore, an ambitious one, but it turned out happy. M. Pougin says:—

Cherubini and his wife, who loved each other tenderly, lived together for forty-eight years in the most perfect harmony, and when the great man died in 1842, not a cloud had ever obscured their constant accord—nothing had been able to alter their mutual affection.

We may state here that of this fortunate and, indeed, blessed union, there were three children—Salvador, who, after a good career as an artist, died in or about 1869;

Victoire, who married a military commissary named Turcas; and Zénobie, who married the well-known artist Rossellini. Madame Cherubini long survived her husband, dying in July, 1864.

More important, in an artistic sense, than the master's marriage, was his enrolment (1794) among the musicians of the National Guard, his instrument, according to D'Ortigue, being the triangle. This may seem rather a degrading position for an eminent man, but the musicians of the National Guard were a peculiar and important body. Originally established in 1789, by a staff-captain named Sarette, as a military band of forty-five players, it had been taken over by the municipality in 1790, and increased to seventy instruments. Then a gratuitous school of instruction was attached to it, which developed (1793) into an Institut National de Musique, comprising 115 artists and 600 students. To this body Cherubini, in his capacity as triangle player, became attached, his more important duties being, of course, those of a teacher. In 1795 the National Guard band was dissolved by decree, the Institut going with it, and a Conservatoire de Musique being established to fill the gap (October 15). Thus arose the famous French school, of which Sarette was the first director, with Grétry, Lesueur, Méhul, Gossec, and Cherubini as inspectors or chief professors. The triangle-player, we may assume, knew what he was about when accepting his humble instrument, though he hardly recognised a first step to the chief place in the most famous of all musical academies.

The events of 1794 include also the production at the Théatre Feydeau of " Elise, ou le Mont Saint-Bernard." This work is generally accounted an exception to the rule that Cherubini's operas are marked by intellectual rather than emotional beauty. It abounds in true Italian melody, of a tender character, and, as the master when writing it was under the influence of his father's death, the fact cannot be deemed surprising. We have more right to be astonished at the opinion of the Parisians, who thought the music " too learned and too German." " Elise " was not the rival of " Lodoiska " in point of success, but Cherubini showed how much he felt inclined to study a light public taste by composing as his next opera " Médée." This, however, was not till near upon two years later, the intervening time being fully occupied with work connected with the new Conservatoire, in which Cherubini taught counterpoint, and in writing solfeggi for use at the same establishment.

In 1797, our master entered upon a novel kind of labour as composer to the Republic. Those were days of national celebrations. France entertained visions of conquest and supremacy. She saw, in anticipation, the world at her feet, and, dating her new life from the dawn of revolution, loved to observe anniversaries and keep alive the memory of great events by magnificent *fêtes*. Into these music of course entered, and Cherubini, who, as a professor at the Conservatoire, received State pay, was sometimes called upon to write patriotic hymns. His biographical notes mention some of these compositions, and from their titles they appear to be of a rather lurid character. There was, for example, an "Ode for the Anniversary of August 18"; and "Le Salpêtre Republicain," performed at a festival in celebration of the manufacture of saltpetre. All, however, were not of this class, something higher and better being found in the "Hymn to Fraternity," the "Festival of Youth," and the "Festival of Gratitude." M. Pougin speaks in high terms of some among them, and calls the "Hymn to Gratitude" superb. We are quite ready to believe his testimony, and can only regret that so much talent should have been wasted upon mere occasional pieces, used one day and for ever laid aside the next. It is not pleasant to dwell upon this episode in Cherubini's life, one which, we cannot help thinking, was thoroughly distasteful to him. As the musical hack of a Republic still reeking from the shambles, he must have despised himself. Happily, nobler work awaited him.

In 1797, Hoffmann flourished as critic of the *Journal des Débats*, but did not confine his labours to journalism. Like most of his class, he wrote libretti, and having already collaborated with Méhul and Nicolo, was anxious to become the colleague of Cherubini. To this end, he prepared a book on the subject of Medea—a theme, as everybody knows, full of gloom and horror, and not at all adapted for the class of lyric drama known as opéra-comique. Nevertheless, Cherubini closed with the musical law-giver of the *Journal des Débats*, and was soon hard at work writing his immortal music. He seems to have laboured with great zeal and assiduity, otherwise the new opera could not have been produced at the Feydeau, on March 13, 1797. We all know

"Médée," and it will be interesting, therefore, to read some of the criticisms passed upon it in connection with the first performance. Some of these are given by M. Pougin, who collected them from dusty files of long-forgotten journals, and deserves thanks for so doing. The *Journal des Indications* said :—

In the part of Medea it—the music—rends the soul ; it paints . . . . The music is broad, expressive, majestic, and terrible.

On its part the *Journal de Paris* remarked :—

Overture, recitatives, duets, and trios in the form of dialogues, concerted pieces, marches, choruses, and accompaniments are all rich in melody and perfectly adapted to the action on the stage.

The *Courier des Spectacles* was not less laudatory, but the *Censeur*, true to its name, declared :—

The music, by Cherubini, is often melodious and sometimes virile, but the public noticed in it reminiscences and imitation of Méhul's manner.

Méhul himself rose up to answer this criticism, and did so in terms of noble generosity. Here is his note to the editor :—

"O *Censeur*, you do not know this great artist. But I do know him, and admire him because I know him well, and I say and will prove to all Europe that the inimitable author of "Démophon," "Lodoiska," "Elise," and "Médée" never required to imitate in order to be successively elegant or tender, graceful or tragic— to be, in a word, that Cherubini whom some few may accuse of imitating others, but whom they themselves will not fail to imitate *unfortunately* at the first opportunity. This justly celebrated artist may find a *Censeur* to attack him, but he will have as defenders all who admire him—that is, all who are capable of understanding and appreciating the highest talent."

Upon this, exit *Le Censeur*, with, it is to be hoped, much shame of face. Upon this also Cherubini dedicated the score to Méhul, in terms as follows :—

Cherubini to Méhul : Receive, my friend, from the hands of friendship the homage she delights in paying to a distinguished artist. Your name placed at the head of this work will lend it a merit it did not possess—namely, that of appearing worthy to be dedicated to you—and this will serve it as a support. May the union of our two names everywhere attest the tender sentiments which bind us to each other, and the respect I entertain for real talent.

Our master had worked so hard at " Médée" that when the opera was safely launched and Mdme. Scio was drawing all the town to see her as the vengeful wife, his health gave way. Rest became necessary and change of scene desirable ; he therefore once more took the diligence to La Chartreuse de Gaillon, and lived for a while with his friends, M. and Madame Louis. A letter written thence to his wife has been published, and is interesting, as showing how tender the so-called "grim Florentine" could be; also, how his pen would slip in writing French.

I have at length received a letter from you, my darling, and hope to receive another to-morrow. I thank you for the pleasure you have procured me, for it is a pleasure to hear about you and my little cocotte (ma petit cocotte). Pretty dear ! so she often asks for me, does she ? Kiss her well for me, as I cannot have the satisfaction of kissing her myself. It is horrible weather here ; nothing but wind and rain. . . . I have not as good an appetite as the first day I came. However, I shall go out to-day after dinner (cette après diner), for the weather is not so bad as it was. Not having " Madame Angot"* to amuse me, I pass my life in eating and sleeping, for we go to bed at half-past ten. We have a little music, and play the remainder of the time; occasionally we have billiards and harmless games in the evening. I am delighted that you also are amused. You are very lucky to be able to go to the first performance of Méhul's piece (" Le Chasse de Jeune Henri"). I shall look forward anxiously for the news of his success. If he achieves such a success as I hope he will and as he deserves, he will have a great one. The only thing that annoys me is not being able to be present at his good fortune, so that I may share it with him, and be the first to tell him what gratification it affords me. . . . Adieu ! Give my dear Victorine, who writes like a little angel, a thousand kisses for me. All the ladies here desire their kind regards ; they wish you had been with me, but that will be some other time. Good-bye, my darling ! With very best love, I remain, your affectionate husband and friend.

There is another letter extant, written to his wife a few days later, but containing little more than small details, of no interest now. Some sentences in it, however, afford a glimpse of the indifference which later on became a feature of hardness in the master's character. They will explain themselves as we quote them :

* A favourite piece then running at the Ambigu.

As for your brother's marriage, I am not at all offended at his contracting it without me. On the contrary, I am glad he spared me the trouble of it. All the worse for him if he is wanting in respect toward his parents. But who were the witnesses at the ceremony? You must tell me all this on my return. Papa sent me a letter, in which he tries to excuse himself for not being able to prevent the solemnisation of his son's marriage without me. I am about to reply to set his mind at ease, and show that my tranquillity is not disturbed by the matter.

Cherubini returned to Paris in May, 1797, and resumed his duties at the Conservatoire, but did little else till the death of that pure-souled patriot, General Hoche, plunged France into mourning. Then, associated with Chenier, he prepared a great lyric scene to be performed at the Opéra and at the Feydeau, in celebration of the departed hero; and thereby hangs a tale.

The death of the Bayard of the Revolution (Hoche) naturally excited in French breasts a desire to honour their lamented hero in a manner the most public and complete. At the Théâtre Feydeau the idea was to prepare a grand lyrical scene by way of *Pompe funèbre*, and thus turn the stage into a place of mourning. Accordingly, Chenier received a commission to write the verses, Cherubini being chosen to compose the music. At this distance of time, and among Englishmen, the ceremonial retains no significance with regard to the connected event, but it gives a curious idea of the sort of thing which served to keep revolutionary and patriotic fervour at white heat among our neighbours many years ago. It opened with a tableau at once realistic and symbolical. Maidens and Old Men in classical attire mixed with officers and soldiers in the military dress of the period. There was a funereal urn; there were offerings of palms and garlands; hymns were sung, drums rolled, muskets fired, and what not beside, of a nature alike stirring and incongruous. The intention was good, no doubt, but the public refused to "take the will for the deed," and one journal said of the piece: "A sort of pantomime; a nullity in point of dramatic merit; it was played simultaneously at two theatres, but did not draw at either." The Hoche *Pompe funèbre* was not to pass, however, without some effect upon the composer of the music. In the result it made an enemy of a young soldier just then rising into power, one who united to vast capacity the meanest and most belittling spirit of jealousy.

The worse than womanish feeling cherished by Napoleon for all rivals is matter of history, and has been proved up to the hilt over and over again. He could even depreciate brilliant services that helped to lay the foundations of his throne, when they overshadowed his own deeds, or promised to make a hero more popular than himself. Desaix, among his subordinates in the campaign of Marengo, and Macdonald, among his marshals in the wars of the empire, had good reason to know what sort of chief they served. Even the grave proved no barrier to the great man's jealousy. Hoche, though dead, still irritated him, and he was impatient of any praise bestowed upon the pacificator of La Vendée. How this unreasonable pettishness affected Cherubini has been set forth by one of the master's biographers, Raoul Rochette, and deserves quotation :—

The conqueror of Arcole brought back from Italy a march of Paisiello's, which he wished to hear at the Conservatoire. The director, M. Sarette, thought he ought to profit by the opportunity and show the young hero, on whom the eyes of all Europe were fixed, the entire resources of the new institution by employing them on a more important composition ; so he selected a cantata and funeral march, written to words by Chénier, by M. Cherubini for the funeral of General Hoche. It is a strikingly expressive piece, containing beauties of the highest order, and had made a prodigious impression on the people of Paris, but failed to do so on the conqueror of Italy. The General felt offended that the performance was not limited to what he had said he should like to hear ; he thought there was an intention to give him a lesson by showing that France could do without foreign talent. Perhaps, too, he was wounded at hearing Hoche's praises sung ; perhaps, in a word, he already desired hymns for no one but himself. Be this as it may, he appeared displeased. Scarcely was the performance over, when he went up to M. Cherubini, and, without saying a word to him about his march, spoke only in praise of Paisiello, whom he looked upon as the first of all composers, while after him he would hear of no one but Zingarelli, which deprived our composer of the hope of taking even second rank. " I say nothing about Paisiello," murmured Cherubini, in a low voice, " but Zingarelli——! " And that was his only answer.

We may add that that only answer Napoleon never forgave. He had a powerful memory for offences against his self-esteem. Cherubini's next work was the one-act opera, "L'Hôtel-

lerie Portugaise," words by an unknown author named
Saint-Aignau, who, somehow or other, had contrived to win
the master's confidence. This work, first played in July,
1798, failed completely, owing to the badness of the libretto,
but the music met with favour at the hands of connoisseurs,
the overture receiving especial praise for reasons which
many readers of these words will not fail to understand.
On his part, Saint-Aignau would not accept the public
verdict as final. He remodelled his book and made another
appeal, but again without success. " L'Hôtellerie Portugaise" struggled through four nights, and then there was an
end of it. Cherubini proved a little more fortunate with his
next opera, " La Punition." Desfaucherets was the author
of the libretto, concerning which the *Courrier des Spectacles*
said : " It has not much in it, is uninteresting, and contains
striking improbabilities." This, too, was remodelled, and
with better results than attended " L'Hôtellerie Portugaise."
Subsequently Cherubini, working with Boïeldieu, brought
out another one-act piece, " Emma, ou la Prisonnière "
(December, 1799), success in its case being—according to
M. Pougin—decided and prolonged, but on the evidence of
authorities accepted by Mr. Bellasis, entirely non-existent.
On which side the truth lies a contemporary newspaper
must be allowed to determine. " ' La Prisonnière,' " said
*Les Spectacles des Paris*, quoted by M. Pougin, " still draws
large numbers to the Théâtre Montansier." All this was
mere prelude to an event of genuine importance—the production of " Les Deux Journées."

The book of " Les Deux Journées" was written by Bouilly,
the literary colleague of Grétry in some of his most important
works, and the betrothed of that master's youngest and most
beloved daughter, Antoinette. Bouilly is described by M.
Pougin as " the wishy-washy and pompous author, whose
pretentious and turgid style might serve as a model for all
Prudhommes, past, present, and future." We shall not
question the judgment nor censure Bouilly's weaknesses,
since his self-importance led him to write a book called
" Mes Récapitulations," wherein we read something of the
genesis of " Les Deux Journées," and learn that the writer
first met Cherubini at the house of Joséphine Beauharnais,
afterwards the wife of Napoleon. At that time the composer
was in search of a good librettist—one who could command
sustained interest in union with new and pleasing situations.

I was happy enough, said Bouilly, to realise his wish. . . . An act of admirable devotion on the part of a water-carrier for the benefit of a friend of mine, a magistrate, who was saved under the Terror as though by miracle, inspired me with the idea of giving the people a lesson in humanity. In a very short time I wrote my piece entitled " Les Deux Journées," and hastened to entrust it to Cherubini. He thought he saw in it something which might afford his rich and fertile imagination all the stimulus he required, and set to work uninterruptedly at composing one of the finest scores of modern times.

After a good deal of vain talk about himself, our librettist goes on to tell what happened at the first performance of " Les Deux Journées." Here he is worth quoting again :—

The overture began and met with general approbation. The first act appeared full of matter well planned and characterised by absorbing interest. Then came the finale, that admirable septet cited as a masterpiece of our modern school. Enthusiasm had reached its highest pitch. Scarcely had the curtain fallen at the end of this act ere a large number of the Conservatoire pupils, climbing up over the orchestra, surrounded their master, who wanted to make me share the congratulations showered upon him. . . . But all my attention was taken up by my water-cart ; the whole fate of the piece depended on that, and on more than one occasion the public have been known to pass from the enthusiasm produced by a first act to great severity as regards the others. I relied with justice on the irresistible spirit of my actor (Juliet); everything had been regulated and measured in order that the scene of the water-cart containing an illustrious personage proscribed by law might produce all the effect we expected ; but a mere nothing might destroy all our hopes : it was necessary that the interest and the comic element in the situation should hit the public at the minute, the second, indicated. The vigilance of a sentinel whose steps were counted had to be eluded. In a word, Count Armand had only a single instant for escape. Everything concurred to make that instant decisive and favourable to the piece. . . . (It) produced on the whole audience one of those outbursts of emotion which cannot be withstood, and which are followed by lasting success. I felt assured from that moment ; and, in my turn, pressing Cherubini in my arms with the eager utterance of deep emotion : " Pardon me, great master ; I trembled, and should never have been consoled had I compromised your fine talent." " Never," he answered, returning my embrace—" no, never, perhaps, shall I have a better occasion for developing it; and I owe you my grandest triumph."

" Les Deux Journées " is so well known to every amateur that a discussion of its characteristics would take up time and space without just cause, while those who wish to learn what some great masters have said about it can gratify their desire by turning to the pages of Mr. Bellasis. From the historical point of view it is more important to show how the opera was received by contemporary critics. We can do this, thanks to the researches of M. Pougin. Here is what the influential *Journal de Paris* said :—

The music of this work is, without doubt, one of its author's masterpieces. Nothing can be more new, more original, and more majestic than the overture ; nothing more dramatic or more finely composed than the finale of the first act ; nothing more simple and more tuneful than the elegant airs scattered through the piece.

The *Courier des Spectacles* remarked : The subject, the situations, the music, and the playing of the actors, all interest us, and deserve the unanimity of general applause which crowned the work . . . . Citizen Cherubini's style of composition is so marked that it is impossible not to know it. Force, rapidity, learned and unexpected transitions, and an accent of deep feeling, which reign in all the passionate situations, are so many signs by which, from the very earliest numbers, we recognise the inimitable author.

On its part the *Année Théâtrale* observed :—

All the sentiments of surprise, joy, disappointment, gratitude, and hope are, in a word, expressed in the tone adapted to them, and the accompaniment always adds to the expression with which the melody is capable of investing them. The whole is blended into a harmonic effect which is one of the richest ever yet heard on the stage.

Taking these opinions in a representative character, it is clear that Cherubini, even in his most individual phase, had not to wait for generous and discerning appreciation. " Les Deux Journées " placed him at once on a pinnacle of the temple of art. The opera, which was produced on January 16, 1800, ran for two hundred nights, and soon found its way out of France into Germany and Italy. In 1801 a much mangled version, bearing the name of Thomas Attwood, was performed in London as " The Escapes," and not till seventy years later did " Les Deux Journées," rise in all its beauty, above our horizon. The opera figured in

D

the Drury Lane season of 1872, recitatives having been written by Sir Michael Costa, but it failed to interest our public. So much the worse, not for it, but them.

*A propos* to "Les Deux Journées," Bouilly tells a curious story, which shows what an impression the work made even upon people far removed from the influence of ordinary operatic doings. One morning twelve water-carriers, one of them bearing a magnificent bouquet, appeared at Bouilly's residence, and said: "Beg pardon, sir, if we intrude, but when the heart speaks it cannot be resisted." Asked to be a little more explicit, the spokesman replied that they came to thank Bouilly, "in the name of all the water-carriers, for the honour you have done us by this masterpiece on the stage, where—blood and thunder!— you have drawn us in such a way that it made us cry, neither more nor less than if we had been a lot of little children." The dialogue continued thus:—

*Bouilly.* I painted you as what you are—worthy and ex- cellent men—and as you deserve to be painted.

*Spokesman.* Well, it all amounts to this—that, in the first place, I have come to beg you will accept these flowers as a mark of our gratitude, and then give us permission—

*Bouilly.* Permission to do what?

*Spokesman.* To supply your house with water for a year, gratis, of course. It is settled with all my mates of this part of the town. Each will have his week. It will be kind of you to do so.

*Bouilly.* I am profoundly touched by your offer, which flatters as much as it honours me. But permit me to accept only these beautiful flowers, which I would not exchange for a crown.

*Spokesman.* O do not refuse us, confound it! That would grieve us too much. Like a good fellow as you are, do not refuse us.

*Bouilly.* Let us say no more on the subject, my good friends. If my piece made your hearts beat, believe me your offer makes mine beat quite as much, and will never be effaced from my memory. As for the flowers, I shall deck my wife and daughter with them, but I promise to keep one which will remind me all my life of this charming interview.

Bouilly adds that he and the water-carriers then drank wine together, and that he preserved one of the flowers beneath a glass shade.

Cherubini next collaborated with Méhul in a three-act opera, " Epicure," which decidedly failed, for reasons that may or may not have been those set forth in a contemporary paper, *Etrennes Lyriques et Théâtrales :—*

Four insignificant personages, opera-like scenes of magic, a hurried ending, the love of a young girl for old *Epicurus*, and the child's confession before the grave *Areopagus* put the spectators in a bad humour and inclined them to laughter. It was time the piece finished when it did. Little interest, but facility of versification ; agreeable touches, but buffoonery for comedy ; interest without interest, but a tolerably satisfactory development of the character of *Epicurus*, which is in itse.f pleasing—such, to our mind, are the beauties and defects of the work. The music is not the music for such a subject : it belongs neither to the buffo nor the terrible style, but makes an infernal noise, produces many orchestral effects, and multiplies difficulties —we do not very well know wherefore. Wishing to surpass each other, the two composers who wrote the music have offered us something scientific for trained ears. The audience were not likely to take this into account.

It is fair to add that this opinion was not shared by many critics, who simply complained that, while each master wrote well, the general effect lacked unity of manner— which, indeed, was to be expected.

The period of " Les Deux Journées " and the " Epicure " was one of great activity on the part of Cherubini. He did not compose much dramatic music, it is true, for some time after the failure of his collaboration with Méhul, and this has deceived some of his biographers into a belief that he was despondent and inactive. M. Pougin gives ample proof to the contrary. We find that Cherubini became connected with a concert speculation at the Théâtre Louvois, in conjunction with Citizens Lefèbvre and Garat. This failed ignominiously, only two performances taking place. A little later the master is discovered in the midst of a hot fight waged between the professors of the Conservatoire and their ex-colleague Lesueur, while about the same time he appears as part editor and proprietor of the *Journal d'Apollon.* M. Pougin has disinterred the advertisement of this publication, and here it is :—

*Journal d'Apollon,* by Citizens Cherubini, Boïeldieu, and Jadin. This periodical will appear under the title of the *Journal d'Apollon.* It will contain new compositions by the three musicians ; each will supply two a month, which, collected, will form six pieces, consisting alternately of French romances, rondeaux, duets and airs, and Italian duets and cavatinas, or canons for three or four voices. The first number will appear on the 1st Floréal next.

M. Pougin adds, in further proof of Cherubini's activity:—

It was also shortly afterwards that Cherubini was mixed up in a commercial scheme, started, doubtless, by several composers to defend their author's rights, disregarded somewhat, probably, by the publishers. One thing, at any rate, is certain—Berton, Boieldieu, Nicolo, Méhul, Jadin, Kreutzer, and Cherubini combined to found a musical publishing firm, in which they traded personally with their own works. The house was situated in the Rue Richelieu, then called the Rue de la Loi; it is the same which Boieldieu's younger brother afterwards took on his own account. The trade-mark of the firm was a star, with the name of one of the associated composers appearing between a couple of the rays.

One of the stories connecting Cherubini with Napoleon comes in about this time, and may be taken with as many grains of salt as the reader pleases. It is said that among the deputations which went up to congratulate the future Emperor upon his escape from Fieschi's infernal machine, was one from the Conservatoire. Cherubini belonged to it, but, knowing Napoleon's prejudice against him, kept in the background. If he hoped thus to avoid remark, he reckoned without his host. The Corsican soldier never forgot anybody, and he soon exclaimed, "I do not see Monsieur Chérubin," using the French rendering of the composer's name. On this Cherubini stepped to the front, and the two men looked at each other, but neither said a word. Another tale follows upon this. Napoleon soon after gave a dinner at the Tuileries to a number of distinguished men, and Cherubini was amongst the guests. On adjourning to the *salon*, the First Consul singled out our master and began, in his restless manner, to walk him up and down the room. He meant to be "nasty," and Cherubini must have detected it, wondering, perhaps, where the blow would fall. "So," said the lord of many legions, "the French are in Italy !" As the Florentine musician was not a very patriotic Italian, this did not hurt him much, and he had no difficulty in turning a compliment out of it. "Where would they not go, led by such a hero as you?"

Napoleon seemed pleased, but soon relapsed into his dis-agreeable humour, and brought up the name of his favourite, Paisiello. " I tell you I like Paisiello's music immensely; it is soft and tranquil. You have much talent, but there is too much accompaniment." Cherubini answered : "Citizen Consul, I conform to French taste; 'paese che vai usanza che trovi,' says the Italian proverb." Napoleon persisted : " Your music makes too much noise. Speak to me in that of Paisiello; that is what lulls me gently." The master's reply showed how unfit he was to figure in courts. Already discerning men saw at what a glittering prize the fortunate soldier was aiming, and Cherubini very plainly hinted it when he replied : " I understand ; you like music which does not stop you from thinking of State affairs." The conqueror's brow darkened ; the hard, stern expression which often made nations tremble settled upon his face, and the conversation ended.

The First Consul soon made a practical retort upon Cherubini. Having re-established religion in France, he revived services at the Tuileries, and, sending for Paisiello, made him director of the music at a salary of 12,000 francs per year. This step naturally irritated the French musicians, and excited their ill-feeling to such an extent that even Cherubini became its object. Napoleon, we may be sure, was not affected by anything they said or did. Retaining Paisiello, as long as that composer would stop—the master returned to Naples in 1804—he revelled in the soothing music of his predilection. Speculation has often concerned itself with the real reasons why Napoleon disliked Cherubini's music and preferred Paisiello's. One writer (Picchianti) quoted by Mr. Bellasis, goes very far afield in search. He argues that the great soldier's nerves, accustomed to the " confused noise " of great armies, could not have found the Florentine's works unbearable by reason of sonority ; and then proceeds :

It is rather to be believed that in Cherubini's music . . . Napoleon discovered the impress of an exalted spirit, and a certain republican austerity, which he did not at all relish, and would have been glad even to eradicate . . . there perhaps arose in him some fear lest such music should produce results clashing with his chief objects, which were to extinguish in the French people all excitement opposed, as he thought, to his particular aims, and for that very reason he wished, on the other hand, to maintain, by means of Paisiello's and Zingarelli's compositions, the reputation of the old school of Italian music, the quiet and suave style of which seemed to him calculated to lull the popular mind.

In our opinion, there is no reason to speculate after this fashion about a fact so perfectly natural as Napoleon's love of soft and soothing music. The man who spends his days amid the whirl of a great city's business loves to retire at night to some quiet suburban retreat, and with equal reason this soldier, accustomed to the din of military bands and the uproar of popular enthusiasm, sought relief in unexciting strains.

In October, 1803, Cherubini appeared for the second time on the stage of the Grand Opéra, where was produced his " Anacréon, ou l'Amour Fugitif." Again he suffered through a bad libretto, his indifference or want of judgment having led him to accept a book from an obscure writer named Mendouze. One might have thought that the master had had experience enough of obscure writers ; but no ; he went on trying to draw a prize blindfold, and always getting a blank, or worse. Castil-Blaze says :

The Anacreonic libretto struck the public as very wearisome and icy cold. They received certain scenes, however, with transports of merriment, especially one in which _Anacréon_, when speaking to his favourite _Odalisque_ to ask her for something to drink, calls her " Esclave intéressante." For five minutes shouts of laughter prevented the actor from going on.

That musicians admired the beautiful overture—played, by the way, at the first concert of our own Philharmonic Society and _twice encored_—as well as many of the solos and concerted pieces, goes without saying, but the public would not have " Anacréon " at any price. For the first time in the annals of the Grand Opéra, they hissed, and the alarmed manager withdrew the work after a run of seven nights.

In December of the following year (1804) Cherubini tried his luck again on the same stage, and once more failed. This time he produced a ballet, " Achille à Seyros," having however, written only a part of the music himself. Ill-fortune attended him in other ways. Paisiello, tired of Paris, left and went home, whereupon Napoleon invited Méhul to take the vacant post at the Tuileries. The French master, it is said, declined in favour of Cherubini ; but several versions of the story are told, and we cannot decide whether he was thus magnanimous or not. According to one authority, the following conversation took place between the Emperor and the composer of " Joseph " :—

*Méhul.* I can only accept the place on condition that you will allow me to share it with my friend Cherubini.

*Napoleon.* Don't mention him ; he is a man of snappish disposition, and I have an utter aversion to him.

*Méhul.* It is certainly his misfortune to have failed in securing your good opinion, but in point of sacred music he is superior to us all ; he is straitened in his circumstances, has a numerous family, and I should feel happy in reconciling you to him.

*Napoleon.* I repeat, I will not have him.

*Méhul.* Well, then, I must positively decline ; nothing can alter my determination. I belong to the Institute ; he does not. I will not allow it to be said that I take advantage of the kindness you show me in order to secure every place for myself and deprive a celebrated man of what he is so justly entitled to claim at your hands.

Castil-Blaze describes all this as pure invention, and the only thing certain is that Napoleon requested Paisiello to name his own successor. Lesueur was the fortunate man.

In 1805 Cherubini organised and conducted a great performance of Mozart's " Requiem." This was his last engagement before quitting the French capital for Vienna, attracted thither by a liberal offer for two operas, to be produced under his personal superintendence. A certain Baron von Braun came from the Kaiserstadt expressly to arrange this affair, and with him Cherubini, his wife, and infant daughter left Paris, travelling by way of Frankfort, Berlin, Dresden, and Prague. The master wrote full details of this long roundabout journey, but little would be gained by quoting from a narrative no more interesting than an ordinary traveller's diary. Enough that the party reached Vienna safe and sound, on July 27, and that Cherubini lost no time in making the acquaintance of the venerable Haydn, then nearing the close of his career ; of Beethoven, whose star was rising towards the zenith ; and of Hummel, then in the glow of his popularity. He soon brought out " Les Deux Journées " and " Lodoïska," and was beginning a new opera for the Vienna stage, when the dark and gigantic shadow of Napoleon fell upon the Austrian capital like an eclipse. Every one knows that in September, 1805, the conqueror broke up the camp of the " Army of England " at Boulogne, and, after one of the most astonishing marches on record, hurled that splendid and irresistible host full at the heart of the Austrian Empire. With magical rapidity he captured Ulm and poor unfortunate Mack, swept on to Vienna, crushed Austria and Russia at Austerlitz, and then returned to the trembling city on the Danube as its master. There he met with Cherubini once more, sending for him and graciously saying, "Since you are here, Monsieur Cherubini, we will have some music together. You shall direct my concerts." This the master did, so pleasing the Emperor that his Majesty one day observed, " I hope that you are here only for a holiday, and intend returning to Paris." A courtier would have known how to " improve the occasion " of this speech, but Cherubini was as proud as Napoleon himself, and made no sign. Otherwise, perhaps, the Florentine, and not Paer, would soon after have enjoyed 50,000 francs a year, with the compound title, " Composer and Director of the Private Musical Establishment of the Emperor, and Singing Master to the Empress."

Cherubini's visit to the Austrian capital, though not unattended by success, could scarcely have equalled his expectations. Everything was upset by the campaign of Austerlitz. For a time the whole fabric of society became disorganised, and this, no doubt, had something to do with the failure of a commercial enterprise in which, according to Picchianti, the master was associated with Steibelt. Lured by the temptations that so often draw artists out of their proper path into bogs and all manner of unpleasant places, the two composers started a music-printing establishment. Of course they did not know how to manage it amid the prevailing confusion, and collapse soon put an end to their anxieties. Cherubini's share of the debts seems to have been a heavy one, but he met it manfully, and for some time had to fight the battle of life with crippled resources. Amid all that was disagreeable in Vienna, Cherubini had some consolation, his " Faniska " being well received and played for twenty-eight nights. The *Allgemeine Musikzeitung* of Leipzig, which had so many curious things to say about Beethoven at this period, noticed the work in due course, remarking :—

The music is in every respect worthy the great master who wrote it ; with the exception of certain passages where he may be reproached with being too artificial; it is profound, full of warmth and power, and thoroughly characteristic. Rich in harmony—sometimes even too much so—it is truly striking and strongly dramatic. But a person must hear it several times to understand and seize it thoroughly.

For reasons already pointed out, Cherubini did not remain in Vienna to produce the second of the two operas he had engaged to write. In his autobiographical sketch we read: "After giving my opera of 'Faniska,' which was performed for the first time February 26, 1806, I started from Vienna on March 9, and arrived in Paris on April 1, after an absence of nine months and four days." It is right to add that "Faniska" was not the only work written at Vienna by our master. In his own catalogue is entered, under date 1805: "March for wind instruments, composed at Vienna for Baron von Braun's private band. A Sonata for barrel organ belonging to Baron Baum."

A great many stories are told about Cherubini's relations with Beethoven, Haydn, and the other less illustrious musicians who then made Vienna a "city of the masters." We shall not here concern ourselves with them. A large proportion is mere fancy, and the game of sifting the chaff from the wheat would not be worth the candle.

Cherubini was received back in Paris with open arms. Especially did the professors and pupils of the Conservatoire greet him who conferred so great a lustre upon the institution he had helped to found. They even organised a musical entertainment of an impromptu sort, whereat was performed sundry selections from his works. *A propos* to this, M. Pougin has placed himself in direct opposition to Fétis on a point which has more than one form of interest. Referring to the extemporised entertainment, Fétis says:—

This protestation on the part of all the distinguished musicians then in Paris, and of the young and warm-hearted students against the imperial disfavour manifested for a great artist, far from being useful to the latter, could only do him harm. The same neglect continued to weigh him down, and his discouragement is marked very significantly in the catalogue of his works, for the years 1806-7-8 mention only fragments of a few pages each. During all this period a frivolous occupation grew to be a passionate pursuit with him, and caused him in some degree to forget music. It consisted in making pen and ink sketches on playing cards, of figures and scenes of which the clubs, spades, hearts, and diamonds formed integral parts. He sometimes used to devote to this work seven or eight hours in a single day. These drawings, which frequently exhibited original fancy, were in much request among his friends, and enabled him to forget his sorrows.

Ferdinand Hiller, writing in *Macmillan's Magazine*, has told us something more of Cherubini's craze for drawing on cards :—

On entering his rooms, the visitors beheld, hung in frames against the walls, a number of pictures of all sizes. Red and black spots were more or less visible here and there, and an attentive examination was needed to account for them. These paintings were the strange productions of a taste that had then become a mania with Cherubini. They represented the most fantastic figures, groups, and scenes, produced by the aid of the hearts and diamonds of playing cards, either entire or divided, according to circumstances. There were dancers with red jerkins, singers with red hats, edifices and landscapes with strange specimens of vegetation, the cards being employed either horizontally, perpendicularly, separately, or in groups, with a greater or less number of pips effaced. It was a means of spending or, perhaps, wasting his time. And yet these combinations of invention and calculation, this victorious search for the solution of voluntarily imposed difficulties were very curious ; and it was impossible not to discover in them a certain analogy with his musical combinations, in which every operation was destined to furnish the secret of a particular phrase, of an effect, or of a long-sustained harmony.

M. Pougin refuses to see in this neglect of music for a fantastic pursuit any sign of discouragement caused by imperial hostility. He holds that the Conservatoire people would not have dared to *fête* Cherubini as a demonstration against Napoleon—which is perhaps true—and he contends that the Emperor's dislike of the composer was not of so pronounced a character as is often represented. In support of this view he quotes a letter from Cherubini's grand-daughter, Madame Clémentine Duret, in which that lady, referring to the skirmishes between the Corsican and the Florentine, says :—

Their conversations, studded with pungent and witty remarks, have been often reproduced, but exaggerated and even misrepresented. In his old age I have heard my grandfather express his surprise at the manner in which phrases, interchanged without any afterthought on either side, between the Emperor and ·

himself, had been reported. " Napoleon was not fond of music,"
he said, "because he did not understand it, and because the
sensation it caused him resembled the effect of a noise which
attacked his nerves and was disagreeable to him. The obligation
he was under of listening to it made him reproach me for the
power of the orchestras I directed. . . . He asked me for
music without common sense, and as I was responsible for the
organisation of the concerts I would not yield to him. He used
then to get impatient at meeting with resistance on my part, and
made cutting remarks which I affected not to take.

M. Pougin further argues that Cherubini's inaction during
the years 1806-8 arose from the cause that operated to the
same end in 1801-2—namely, nervous disease :—

The nervous affection to which he was always subject, and
which frequently exerted a baneful influence, not on his disposition
—for he was at bottom good and kindly—but on his temper,
sometimes manifested itself in painful and cruel paroxysms.

All these observations are worth taking into account, but,
on considering the whole matter, we are inclined to think
with Fétis rather than with the later biographer. On the
one hand, the evidence of Napoleon's prejudice against
Cherubini is too strong to be much weakened by testimony
like that of Madame Duret, while the nervous sensitiveness
of the master's organisation would cause him to feel with
special keenness a slight like the preferment of Paër over
his head. The devotion of Cherubini to absurd card-
drawings favours a belief that he suspended musical work
out of sheer disgust. A man whose nervous system has
broken down does not take to labour of any kind for seven
hours a day—he is usually restless and aimless ; whereas a
man who feels that serious exertion meets with no reward
is apt to take up with odd and useless pursuits as a kind of
protest against the injustice that declines to recompense
any other. That Cherubini fretted himself into a state
of nervous disorganisation is likely enough. The card-
drawing was only occupation for his fingers, and his soul
rebelled against the very relief it sought. Happily, a way
of escape out of the Slough of Despond was opened up.
In 1808 our master accepted an invitation to spend a holiday
with the Prince and Princess of Chimay, at their castle
in Belgium. From this mere accident, so to speak, sprang
great and enduring results.

Cherubini's health soon began to improve under the influence of country air and change of scene; but no one pressed him on the subject of music, and for a while he continued to keep aloof from his art, preferring to study botany when rambling about the estate. Matters stood thus as St. Cecilia's Day drew near, and the heads of a musical society in the village were debating what work should be performed at the festival of their patroness. Some one of those heads—we wish his name was known, since the world is his debtor—suggested an application to the great composer at the castle. The idea was a bold one, but the simple villagers acted upon it at once. They found Cherubini, and humbly begged him to write a mass for Chimay church, he listening, though all the while busily arranging some botanical specimens. The answer was "short, sharp, and decisive "—" No; it's impossible." More than this he refused to say, and the deputation, after standing awhile in painful confusion, silently retired with no very high opinion, it may be, of Cherubini's good manners. Perhaps Cherubini had no very high opinion of them himself, and hastened to make atonement; but, anyhow, the interview quickly bore fruit. On the morrow the master seemed preoccupied, took a longer walk than usual, and on returning found a sheet of music paper on his desk, placed there by the watchful princess. In this case it might be said, "Full oft the sight of means to do good deeds makes good deeds done." Cherubini at once sat down and wrote the "Kyrie" of his Mass in F, only getting up now and then to take a turn at the billiard table. This was the beginning of that wonderful series of masterpieces which he gave to the Church. "Behold, how great a matter a little fire kindleth!"

Auber was staying at Chimay, and at his suggestion the new "Kyrie" was at once tried, himself presiding at the pianoforte, while Cherubini sang bass, the Prince tenor, and a lady visitor soprano. General admiration encouraging the composer to go on, he soon completed a "Gloria," both "Kyrie" and "Gloria" being subsequently performed in the village church, with the aid of a real village band, comprising a quartet of strings, horns, clarinets, a flute, and a bassoon. The rest of the work our master composed on his return to Paris, and the first performance took place (1809) at the Prince de Chimay's hotel. Fétis, who was amongst the guests on that occasion, wrote:—

Never shall I forget the effect produced by this Mass confided to such interpreters. All the celebrities of Paris, of whatever rank they might be, attended the performance, where the glory of the great composer shone forth with a living lustre. During the interval between the performance of the " Gloria " and that of the " Credo " groups everywhere formed themselves, and all expressed an unreserved admiration for this composition of a new order, whereby Cherubini has placed himself above all musicians who have as yet written in the concerted style of church music.

As we are here concerned in the events of Cherubini's life, not with the significance of his works, there is no place for discussion as to the claims of dramatic church music, which derived so immense an impetus from the genius of the Florentine master. It suffices to contemplate the apparently insignificant series of circumstances that led Cherubini back again into the paths of art, and induced him not only to make a fresh start, but to direct his course along a new path.

Not long after his return to Paris, Cherubini received the news of Haydn's death, and referred to the event in a letter addressed (June 19, 1809) to Neukomm. His words of regret for the old master's departure are worth transcribing:

You spoke about our dear Father Haydn. We have just received the sad intelligence of his death. He ceased to exist three days after the date of your letter, for it was on May 31 that we lost him. You little thought, no doubt, dear sir, that he was dying when you were speaking to me about him, and he expired while your letter was on its road to me. It is a sad misfortune that this great man is no more, but it is a blessing for him, since he has ceased to suffer, for he had been very long time a martyr. Music loses much. She has still his works left, but it is a great misfortune that he can write no more of them, and that no one is left who can replace him.

Cherubini ، paid a much better tribute than this to the *manes* of his illustrious brother in art. In 1805, Haydn being then seriously ill, report reached Paris that he had died, whereupon Cherubini composed an appropriate hymn, for three voices and orchestra, in honour of the supposed defunct. The work had, of course, to be put aside as soon as it was found that Haydn still lived ; but when his death actually took place, four years later, it was brought forward and performed at a concert given by the pupils of the Con-

servatoire. Great attention seems to have been excited by
the music. It was performed a second time, and then a
Parisian critic spoke as follows :—

The introduction of this fine composition is of a sombre and
religious tinge ; the violoncello, double basses, flutes and horns
play a mournful strain, which plunges the soul into a state
of dark melancholy and sorrowfully presents us with the mage
of Death, whose cruel scythe spares neither genius, wealth,
youth, nor beauty. . . . Haydn is no more. . . . The
Nymph of the Danube bewails the death of the great man whose
divine talent adorned the river banks, two shepherds offer her
consolation based on the immortal glory of Haydn, whose genius
and works will live for ever after him. Such is the substance
of this funeral scene, whence M. Cherubini has derived the
richest effects of harmony and melody. The manner in which
he has depicted the charm of Haydn's pure strains is so truthful
that we might almost believe the music to be written by Haydn
himself; he has imitated with great art one of the happiest
phrases in the oratorio.

The hymn was subsequently published with a dedication
to Prince Esterhazy, Haydn's patron and master, who
politely acknowledged the honour, at the same time for-
warding a snuffbox ornamented with gold and diamonds.

Thoroughly restored to health and work, Cherubini composed " Pimmalionè," a one-act Italian opera, which was
produced (November 30, 1809) at the theatre in the Tuileries
before the Emperor and Empress. Upon this event M.
Pougin bases another argument against the reported feud
between Napoleon and the Florentine, but we need not here
reopen the subject. It is more to the purpose to note that
having written an ode for the marriage of the Emperor with
Marie Louise (May 20, 1810) he brought out at the Opéra-
Comique (September 1, 1810) a one-act buffo opera, entitled
" Le Crescendo." Again the musician suffered for the sins
of the librettist. A contemporary critic wrote :—

The plot, though tolerably well worked out, appeared devoid
of interest and even of comicality. . . . A discontented spectator
allowed a slight hiss to escape his lips ; his neighbours fell foul
of him ; he retorted by saying he had been bored for some time,
and wanted to amuse himself a little by hissing. His reason was
heard and backed up by others who also were bored. The heresy
that a man must hiss when he is bored made rapid progress, and
this produced a *crescendo* of hisses as fatal to the piece as the
*crescendo* of music was to the Baron.

On its merits, the music of "Le Crescendo" met with universal approval, but, as Garaudé pointed out at the time, "musical beauties alone are not sufficient in an opera offered to a French audience, who require, in addition to these, reasonable action, a piquant plot, and novel situations, or, at least, a story that shall fix the spectator's attention by the natural and probable connection of scenes attractive by their gaiety or interest." The same writer continued as follows :—

The French want a complete whole, and M. Cherubini has proved more than once that he can successfully supply it. How is it that, on the present occasion, he has profaned his genius by associating it with such a rhapsody ? On reflecting, we might return more than one answer to this question. In the first place, had he a choice ? Are good works so common ? May he not have thought that an innovation of this nature would be welcomed by the public ? And is the taste of the public so sure that we may reasonably guarantee its infallibility ? Who are the literary men and composers that would dare to predict with assurance the failure or success of an opera ?

These questions are not worth much as excusing Cherubini's repeated mistakes in the matter of libretti, the merits of which he seemed quite incapable of appreciating, and so took good or bad with perfect submission to the whims of chance. From a letter of the master dated December 12, 1810, he appears to have begun an opera entitled "Nausicaa," and there gives reasons to the author, one Toug, why he felt unable to complete it. The year 1811 was almost a blank, save for the Mass in D minor—an important qualification truly—written between March and October, while in 1812 Cherubini did even less; only one composition—a cantata for some convivial occasion—appearing in his catalogue. It was during this year, however, that he began "Les Abencérages," the book of which had been written, from Florian's "Gonsalve de Cardone," by Jouy. The old story, now grown tiresome, here repeats itself. Jouy's libretto turned out to be as bad as the rest, while the music, though redeemed by the fine overture and some concerted pieces, did not come up to Cherubini's usual mark. Under these circumstances success could not be hoped for. The opera struggled on for twenty nights ; was then withdrawn to be condensed into two acts, and appeared no more.

The great political and national crisis which marked the fall of Napoleon did not fail to touch Cherubini personally.

As soon as France realised what had happened on the blood-stained fields of Germany, and heard a banded Continent thundering at her gates, the men in power adopted every imaginable device for the purpose of stimulating patriotism. Amongst other things they revived the practice of the Republican days, and ordered the preparation of plays and spectacles intended to excite martial ardour. These were hurriedly compiled, generally by two or three authors in collaboration, and as hastily put upon the stage. One opera, in two acts, entitled " Bayard á Mézières," was the joint production of no less than six authors—that is to say, two librettists and four composers, of whom Cherubini was one. This work was produced at the Opéra-Comique on February 12, 1814, and we learn of it from Cherubini's own catalogue that our master's share therein was a trio, a con-certed piece, and a martial song. A journalist of the period states that " Bayard á Mézières," though composed " by order of the police," had a great success, and that Cheru-bini's air was " full of energy and originality." According to M. Pougin, Cherubini wrote, also, a war-song for a drama, " La Rançon de Duguesclin," by Arnault, brought out at the Comédie-Française on March 17. It was not alone as a stage composer that Cherubini contributed his share to the stirring circumstances of the time. The Government having revived the National Guard, a band was organised for it, the musicians being entirely supplied by the Conservatoire. This event was chronicled as follows in the *Journal des Débats* of February 18, 1814:—

Zeal for the National Guard is manifested among all classes ; the artists, never backward when called upon to display their devotion, have just given another proof of it. On the invitation of the Prefect of the Seine and the general staff, the members of the Imperial Conservatoire have formed among themselves a company of 120 volunteer musicians. The director commands it ; the lieutenants are MM. Méhul, Cherubini, Cotel, and Paël. The distinguished wind-instrumentalists trained in the institution, united with the professors, constitute the body of 120 performers.

A very notable band, indeed, this must have been, and no doubt Lieutenant Cherubini was proud of it. As a matter of course, he helped to provide new music. His catalogue speaks of a March and a Double Quick composed for the 120 patriots; but a curious commentary upon Lieutenant Cheru-bini's own zeal for France is that the same catalogue records, only a little later, the issue of a number of military pieces at the request of the colonel of a Prussian regiment. Well, the master, after all, had only adopted France as his mother land. It should also be remembered that he had no particular reason to identify himself with Napoleon's cause. Hence he was quite ready to write for the Prussian colonel, and, as happened directly after the restoration of the monarchy, to compose cantatas in honour of the Bourbon King. For him art had neither politics nor nationality. Cherubini prepared two Restoration Cantatas; one, in three parts with accompaniment, for a military *fête* given on July 20; the other —for several voices, with choruses and accompaniments— being performed before the King on August 29. More important than all these things put together was a work bearing the same date. In 1814 our master composed his first string quartet (E flat) the refined and classic beauty of which, if it needed a foil, would find one in its author's warlike effusions.

The Government of Louis XVIII. was not slow to mark Cherubini's worth by official honours, which had been denied him by the unforgiving Napoleon. In December, 1814, the master was gazetted Chevalier of the Legion of Honour, and in the same month he succeeded M. Martini as Superintendent of the King's musical establishment. Nevertheless, all things did not run quite smoothly under the new *régime*. The Government played havoc with the Conservatoire ; dismissing its founder and director, Sarette, under circumstances of positive contumely, and so disorganising the establishment that Cherubini found himself without anything to do. Under these circumstances an invitation came to him from England, which he at once accepted. Just then the London Philharmonic Society was in the full flush of youthful vigour. It had been founded by Cramer, Clementi, Neate, and their fellows, less than two years before, and naturally desired to achieve something of a sensational nature. Hence the invitation to Cherubini, who was the first to receive a compliment afterwards accepted by Beethoven, Spohr, Weber, Mendelssohn, Wagner, and Gounod. In our master's case the offer was to compose two works, and conduct them himself. These pieces took the form of an overture and a symphony; but Cherubini also wrote a vocal composition, which, together with several selections from his repertory, were duly performed. According to his diary, he started for London on February 25, 1815, and returned to Paris on June 8.

E

Admirers of Cherubini are indebted to M. Pougin for much further information concerning the master in London than was available before the appearance (1882-3) of his articles in *Le Ménéstrel.* Mr. Bellasis, who for the purpose of his biography consulted all known authorities, was driven to dismiss Cherubini's second experience in this country with less than a couple of pages. Within that limited space, however, he presents a translation of an Italian letter, which appears not to have been before published. It is undated and addressed to a Mr. S. Vestri, 6, Rupert Street, Haymarket. Mr. Vestri was, from the terms of the note, collaborating with his illustrious countryman—probably upon the pastoral cantata " Inno alla Primavera," and, like most of his tribe, had failed to keep up a proper supply of " copy." The master writes to hurry him on :—

Most esteemed Signor Vestri,—Well, I shall expect your work to-morrow morning without fail. I hope you will do me the favour of coming to me, or of letting me know whether I am to go to you. I warn you that I shall be unable to wait longer for those words, as the Philharmonic Concerts are going to conclude, and this piece must be ready for the last, which will take place shortly. Believe me, as I have the pleasure of signing myself, your affectionate friend and servant, L. CHERUBINI.

M. Pougin also prints letters of Cherubini for the first time, but they are of real and high importance, because originally conveying to the master's wife, who remained in France, interesting particulars of his London doings. Unfortunately, the French biographer does not possess the complete set. Cherubini reached London at the end of February, whereas the first printed letter bears date March 22, and it is otherwise evident that he had not neglected to write earlier. The letter just referred to begins with a long account of the circumstances under which Madame Cherubini's third and fourth epistles to her husband reached his hands in inverted order, the fourth coming before the third. Incidentally therefrom we learn that he " dined at the house of Mr. Broadwood, with Erard's son, who was one of the party," Cramer also being present ; and that on the same evening, he went to the Opera, "where I felt thoroughly wearied, so bad was it." Another paragraph has more interest, and should be transcribed entire :—

Do not be afraid, my dear, of writing at too great length. I am too eager for your letters and for news about you not to relish them deliberately, however long they may be. I have no patience to read long epistles from those for whom I do not care, but I take a pleasure in perusing from beginning to end those of persons whom I cherish. I am now in the midst of dinner parties and society, where I am very well received and petted. The day before yesterday I went to a grand dinner given me by Braham, the best singer in London, and husband of Madame Storace,* whose portrait you saw at that good creature Haydn's. The dinner was given with several directors of the Philharmonic Concerts. H.R.H. the Duke of Sussex, one of the king's sons, a great musical amateur, very affable, and altogether a good fellow, was present. He would have me placed next him at table, and was exceedingly amiable. We drank like fishes, and remained three hours and a half at table. At ten o'clock we had coffee ; we then played whist, and left at half-past twelve.

From this truly convivial subject the letter turns to business. Cherubini had in view a benefit concert, and he speculates as to the amount it will bring him in :—

I think that if the place is full at half a guinea each—and that price cannot be increased without making people cry out—the receipts will amount to 250 or 300 guineas, from which must be deducted the unavoidable expenses. It is better to give the concert in the Philharmonic Rooms than in the Opera House concert-room, which is much larger, and would drag me into greater expenses. Whatever the concert may bring me in will be so much profit, and many a mickle makes a muckle. If at the end of my visit, I give " Le Mont St. Bernard " at the Opera House, I think I shall make £700, or a little more. That should be in French money about 14,000 francs.†

The letter ends with a reassuring sentence for the anxious wife whose husband was in the midst of temptation: "Adieu, my dear, I am as good as gold."

Cherubini wrote again on April 7. The Hundred Days had then begun, and communication with France was exceedingly difficult. Letters, however, could be smuggled from one country to the other through Belgium, and in this way the master and his wife contrived to correspond. The circumstances were exceedingly unpleasant all round, as the following paragraph shows :—

* This must be an error. Madame Storace's husband was Fisher, the violinist, who, though he disappeared long before 1815, was not known to be dead.

† M. Pougin corrects Cherubini's arithmetic, and points out that £700 makes about 18,000 francs, which is, of course, right.

You reproach me with not often writing to you; your complaint is not well founded, since I have sent you eight letters to your six. Were I sure that the letters would go by the ordinary way, I would write to you oftener; but, being uncertain, I write only when I am sure my letters will go. A time will come when I shall not be able to hear from you nor you from me. This is a distressing prospect, and grieves me very much. Besides this apprehension, I have that of not knowing what road I shall be able to take when I wish to return to France. M. Sorbet told me that, when he is obliged to go back, in six weeks' time, he fears he shall be compelled to reach the Continent by the coast of Spain. Fancy my being obliged to do the same ! What a terrible and what a long journey!

There is next a reference to some negotiations going on between himself and a Prussian Count as to a matter awaiting notice in its place. From this Cherubini passes to his London concerns :—

Last Monday they played my new overture (in G) at the Philharmonic Concert ; it was very successful, and they had it over again. They also sang the "Incarnatus est" from the three-part Mass, and that also had to be repeated. Despite this success, I foresee that my journey here will be a failure ; I expect hardly any profit from it. We have reckoned up the expenses, and they come to 100 guineas. If I have not a full house I risk, after taking a great deal of trouble, gaining only fifty guineas, if, indeed, I am not something out of pocket. Money runs away here like water, and the slightest things are proportionately dear. The outlay will amount to so much, since I shall not be able to have more than three parts of the band without paying them. There is no longer any idea of the opera of "Eliza"; this is why I consider my journey a failure, and, had I foreseen such a result, I should certainly not have undertaken it, for I should at least have received in Paris the net sum of £200, which, as things now stand, is broken in upon and pledged for my travelling and living here. All this clouds my soul, and I am so affected by it, so sad, that, with the work I am obliged to do, if I do not fall ill it will be a miracle. Already my health, which up to now has been good, is becoming bad ; for several days *my nerves have been ill*, and I suffer from a melancholy which I cannot overcome. All this troubles, consumes, and wears me away.

M. Pougin adds that the English climate had undoubtedly a bad effect upon Cherubini's health, and that, after returning to Paris, he suffered for three years from a nervous affection. Our climate is a trying one, granted ; but if gentlemen come' here from more abstemious countries, sit three hours and a half at dinner, and drink like fishes, what can they expect ?

Mention has been made of a negotiation going on between Cherubini and a certain Prussian nobleman. The distinguished individual in question was Count von Bruhl, Chamberlain of Frederic William's Court, and Intendant of the Royal Theatres. He had been commissioned by his master to organise the Court music on a fitting scale, and his natural desire was to obtain the services of an eminent composer. He thought at once of Cherubini, whom it would be a double pleasure to secure, since the gain of Berlin meant the loss of Paris. Count Bruhl forthwith wrote to Cherubini in the French capital—not knowing that the master was on the other side of the Channel—and asked him his terms for the following duties : To write two operas each year ; to conduct them, and, alternately with the second director, to conduct grand operas by foreign composers ; to conduct a Court concert when ordered by the King ; and, in case a Conservatory should be established, to act as one of the professors. The Count graciously added :— " Everything shall be done to please and content you." And then, like a frugal German: " I only trust that the pecuniary conditions may not be such as place too many obstacles in the way of the treasury of the Theatre Royal."

Cherubini received this letter in London, as we already know, and it seems to have presented a difficulty. He was, of course, doubtful of his position in France, Napoleon having regained the throne. There was a possibility of Louis XVIII. returning, in which case the Berlin appointment would not be needed. On the other hand, the Emperor might hold his ground, and then Cherubini would be glad of such a position. Under these circumstances the master's reply to the Count was adapted to delay a conclusion till the imminent struggle between Napoleon and the Allies should have been determined. As a means to this end, Cherubini's letter is skilful. In the first place, he questioned whether, under the altered political circumstances, the offer still held good :—

Were the proposal which you made me before this state of things still to be made, sir, would you make it now ? Unless you have the kindness to reassure me, I fear, in this storm, to accept an engagement which might afterwards be broken by the force of circumstances. Do you not therefore think, M. le Comte, that it would be better to wait till the tempest is over before proceeding with what you propose ?

The master then went on to say that he must remain faithful to his French engagement, which was not hopelessly lost, but that he did not decline the Count's, only asking to have it left in abeyance for awhile. On the point of terms, Cherubini asked a salary of 16,000 francs a year (£640), his professorship at the projected Conservatorium to be an extra, as at Paris, where he received 5,000 francs, with a residence. He also desired travelling expenses for himself and family, and 2,000 francs down a month before leaving Paris.

When, a few weeks later, the battle of Waterloo—

On that loud Sabbath, shook the spoiler down,

there was an end to all palaver with Berlin. The stupid Bourbons went lumbering back to Paris, and Cherubini remained faithful to his French allegiance. He went home gladly, and on the way experienced all the miseries of old fashioned travel in sailing boats and diligences. This we know from a letter written at Calais to his wife, and dated June 5, eight a.m. Therein we read—and reading, are thankful for the days of steam—as follows :—

I quitted London at half-past five, and, after travelling all night, arrived at Dover at nine in the morning. I made the indispensable arrangements with regard to passports and luggage, then I took my place on board a French packet which was to start in the afternoon for Calais. At half-past six I went on board ; the weather was very favourable, but the wind extremely high, which made me as sick as a pig during all the passage, which began at seven o'clock, and we entered the port of Calais at ten in the evening. Not being at that hour able to enter the town, which was closed, we slept on board the packet, and at six o'clock in the morning of to-day the commissary came to examine our passports. . . . About ten they will examine the luggage. . . . The diligence leaves here every day, and if the luggage could have been examined before the hour of its departure, I should have been able to set out to-day. But as that cannot be, on account of the Custom House, I shall not start before to-morrow ; and on Thursday, about eleven, I shall arrive in Paris.

· The master concludes :—

Good-bye, my dear. I can scarcely contain myself for joy at being near the moment of embracing you all after so much bother and anxiety with regard to my affairs and our correspondence. Farewell, my darlings ; we shall soon see each other again.

It should be mentioned here that Cherubini was returning to Paris as a member of the Institute, having been elected in his absence. Here, also, it may be mentioned that his English works were three—an Overture in G, a Symphony in D (the themes of which were subsequently used for the Quartet in C), and the " Hymn to Spring," of which mention has already been made. None of these had a great success then or later, wherefore the master's second visit to London cannot be accounted as a brilliant episode in his career.

On arriving in Paris Cherubini at once resumed his commanding position. The Florentine's genuis was the greatest that France then possessed, and when important work had to be done he was sought as a matter of course. Hence we learn from his Diary that in August, 1815, he composed a " Chorus and Couplets for the Festival of St. Louis"; also that (January 29, 1816) he wrote a " Cantata for several voices with chorus and full band " for the banquet given by the Royal Guard to the National Guard on February 5. Nevertheless, the master's position was by no means satisfactory at this time. The Napoleonic Conservatoire met with little favour from the restored government, who not only changed its name to " Royal School of Music and Declamation," but reduced its allowance to 80,000 francs, dismissed all the professors suspected of attachment to the late *régime*, and cut down the salaries of those who, like Cherubini, were retained. Our master, however, managed to better himself. As Inspector of Instruction and Professor of Composition, Cherubini had been, since 1812, in the receipt of 5,000 francs a year. The Bourbon ministers reduced this to 3,000 by abolishing the first-named office, and from that small amount took off three per cent. to provide a pension. On the other hand, Cherubini received an annual 1,600 francs as a member of the Institute, and two yearly allowances from the King of 2,000 francs and 800 francs respectively. These amounts brought his salary up to 7,400 francs, or £296. The master was at this time fifty-six years old, and

it is hardly to be wondered at that Fortune thought the
hour had come in which to do him a good turn. This she
accomplished by removing from earthly life Martini, the
Superintendent of the King's music, of whose post, valued
at 6,000 francs per annum, Cherubini held the reversion.
We take the particulars concerning this matter from M.
Pougin, by whom it is shown that Castil-Blaze, and,
necessarily, all who have copied him, including Mr. Bellasis,
are wrong when they say, " M. Lesueur, Director of Napoleon's Chapel, became Superintendent of Louis XVIII.'s,
and shared the sceptre of harmony with an illustrious
colleague, Cherubini." In the first place, Lesueur was
not Louis XVIII.'s chapel-master, though he had been
Napoleon's. This M. Pougin conclusively proves by an extract from the official *Moniteur* for February 18, 1816, in
which we read, after an announcement of Martini's death :
" M. Cherubini, who had the reversion, succeeds to the
place as master of the music of the chapel." If it be asked
how Martini came to supersede Lesueur, the answer is that
the Bourbons were accustomed to sell the place, and that,
in Louis XVI.'s time, Martini bought the reversion for
16,000 livres. Of course the bargain had no force during
the Republic and Empire, but as soon as Louis XVIII.
appeared on the scene, Martini claimed his right, and
Lesueur was dismissed to make room for him. How
Cherubini obtained the reversion in turn does not appear,
but there is evidence to show that his appointment took
place the very day after Martini's death. In the oft-quoted
Diary we read :—

I did duty with the Royal choir, in the place of M. Martini, ill,
February 2, 1816. Martini died February 14, 1816, at five
o'clock p.m., and on Thursday, the 15th of the same month, I
was appointed to the post of Superintendent.

This raised his salary to nearly 14,000 francs, or £560,
and relieved him from all anxiety with regard to means of
living.

Cherubini's promotion had a most important effect upon
his future career as a composer. It took him away from the
operatic stage, for which he afterwards wrote but one work
of any consequence, and it turned the current of his genius
in the direction of the Church with a force and steadiness
before unknown. It becomes desirable, therefore, to know

something of the conditions under which the master entered upon his new place. He found, we are told, an orchestra and choir "whose equal, perhaps, no other place in Europe could then show." The singers comprised twelve *soli* and thirty-nine chorus voices; there were fourteen violins— played by, amongst others, Baillot, Habeneck, and Kreutzer —four violas, six violoncellos, four double-basses, flutes, oboes, clarinets, trombones, bassoons (two of each), three horns, two harps, and drums. Two pianists and as many organists were also in the *personnel* of this really royal band.

It is much to be regretted that Cherubini was not allowed to write as he pleased for the King's fine choir. Louis XVIII., despite abundant reason to feel thankful and devout, did not love long religious services. The shorter they were the sweeter he found them, and his new chapel-master was under obligation to bear the fact in mind. Hence, the number of short masses composed by Cherubini subsequent to his appointment, and also the many fragments written in order that at least one movement might be properly developed. One of the complete masses due to this period is the " Requiem " for four voices and orchestra, performed at an anniversary of Louis XVI.'s death. Contemplation of this work opens up the whole question—if question be the right word—of Cherubini's greatness as a religious composer. As to the "Requiem " itself two very different men have spoken—Fétis and Ferdinand Hiller. The one says :—

Although we may object, perhaps, that the " Dies iræ " is too noisy and its forms too dramatic, the art with which the whole is written is so remarkable, and all the other numbers are at one and the same time of so noble and so melancholy a character, that we may class the work among the finest its author ever wrote. The last number, in which he has expressed, with as much simplicity as depth, the exhaustion of all vital sentiment and the entering into eternal repose, impresses the heart, and strikes it with terror.

On the same subject Hiller writes :—

While speaking of Cherubini's sacred works, I must mention one which may undoubtedly be called the most perfect of all— the " Requiem" he composed for the anniversary of Louis XVI.'s death. This is a work almost unique in music. It is possible that Cherubini may not have reached in it the ideal beauty or the profundity of thought and sentiment which we find in certain

pages of Mozart's "Requiem." But, as we know, that
"Requiem" was not completed by its divine author, all the
parts are not equally elevated, and the style wants the finished
unity which gives even secondary ideas the elevated character
they ought to have. In Cherubini's work it appears that everything as far as the words will admit, is developed out of the
eternal lamentation "Dust thou art ; to dust thou shalt return."
What ardent supplication ! What depth of lamentation ! What
dread of the Last Judgment ! And how, at the end, life appears
to be annihilated in one long moan ! In the fugue on the words
recalling the promise made to Abraham and his race, the daring
contrapuntist rouses himself, and not only asserts his rights, but
obstinately claims them ; the episode being, perhaps, necessary
in order that the effect of the work might not be too terrific.
This composition is truly surprising from the simplicity of the
means employed, the colour of the instrumentation, and the
truly vocal manner in which the voices are treated. Had
Cherubini left nothing else, this alone would suffice to place
every true musician under the obligation of considering him as
the most extraordinary and the most sublime of composers.

This is high praise, but few who have made careful study
of Cherubini's sacred works will care to contest it. They
see in them not only the consecration of great genius to
religion, but consecration under the guidance of sound
judgment. Cherubini's masses are free with an ordered
freedom, and they exemplify the fact that a truly great
composer is the master of his art, not its slave, and that to
exercise a judicious liberty he need not rise in insurrection
against rule. The critic last quoted writes :—

The fruit of the severe studies to which he had so constantly
devoted himself in his youth was now apparent in all parts of
his music, and, while he employed every modern harmonic license,
that music preserved at bottom a character of austerity which,
like leaven, imparted to the composition a healthy mordant.

Referring again to the "Requiem" for Louis XVI., it may
be interesting to add that the work was appointed for performance at the funeral of Boieldieu, in 1834, but could only
be given in the Chapel of the Invalides—a place out of
episcopal jurisdiction—because the then Archbishop of Paris,
like Cardinal Manning in our own day, forbade women to
sing in choirs. Cherubini was much annoyed at this, and
said :—

Very well, then ; since they have resolved that women's voices shall not be heard in a church, I will write for my own funeral a " Requiem" against which they shall have no objection.

This he did, and the second "Requiem," for three-part male choir and orchestra, was duly performed over his body. Cherubini, by the way, attended Boieldieu's obsequies, and made a speech at his grave. This has, happily, been preserved—happily not less for the orator than for his subject, since it shows what real generosity and frank appreciation the master could show towards the memory of a fellow-artist. We make no apology for quoting a few sentences :—

To-day we have to weep over Boieldieu, my very dear friend, whose death will be for us a never-ending source of regret. I was long connected by the bonds of friendship with this kindly man, with this composer of distinguished genius. I saw him first enter on his musical career, in which he proceeded from one success to another. I will not now mention the admirable works he composed. They are immortal ; we all know and shall never forget them. . . . I cannot refrain from expressing the deep grief I feel at his death. I have lost a friend and a brother, of whom I shall have nothing left but a sorrowful recollection. . . . Farewell, Boieldieu, farewell ! I preceded you in life and in the career you so nobly followed, yet I now regret you, and weep over the earth about to close upon you, for God has chosen to call you to Him before me.

The year of Cherubini's appointment as chapel-master was one of remarkable fecundity. Besides the " Requiem" already mentioned, the composer wrote the Mass in C (No. 6), nine Kyries, a Laudate, a Sanctus, an O Salutaris, the Mass in E flat (No. 7), several hymns, a cantata (" Le Mariage de Salomon "), and a Lauda Sion. Considering the age at which Cherubini had arrived, this list shows the enthusiasm with which he entered upon his duties and the real devotion he bore to art. Actual production, however, does not represent all his labour. In order to fit himself for Church writing he made careful studies of Palestrina, even going so far as to copy out a number of his works, transposed into other keys, so that the old master's method might become thoroughly familiar. Thus, with all his genius, did Cherubini plod, and only by plodding can genius of any kind reach the highest position. Pegasus is all very well, but his wings are not strong enough for the loftiest place.

In the course of his interesting and valuable biography of Cherubini, M. Arthur Pougin regards the master's appoint-

ment to the King's Chapel as the beginning of a new stage
in his career, and pauses therefore to deal with certain
matters important to a fair understanding of his character.
We gladly pause, likewise, because the French writer
furnishes us with some really important information on a
point as to which considerable misapprehension may prevail.
Cherubini is frequently spoken of as the "stern Florentine,"
and set down as a hard, uncouth man, with few loves and
many hates.  For this Berlioz is partly responsible, through
holding up the Italian musician to ridicule and contempt
in his famous autobiography.  It is remembered against
Cherubini, moreover, that he refused or neglected to answer
Beethoven when written to regarding the Missa solennis
in D, while not a few stories are current, all tending to
the same unfavourable conclusion.  We do not dispute the
existence of some ground for the prevailing idea.  Cherubini
had a temper like most men, and was particularly impatient
of incompetence and presumption.  His manner, too, was
wanting in French polish, and the occasions were many in
which he spoke the truth without periphrasis.  Yet there
is ample evidence to prove that he had a kind and gentle
heart—that he was capable of loving and, therefore, obtained
the love of others.  We now ask the reader to accept some
portion of the testimony in question.

Cherubini's intimacy with Méhul has already appeared
in the course of these remarks.  The terms in which he
dedicated his "Medée" to the composer of "Joseph," and
in which, when writing to his wife from London, he referred
to his friend and colleague, cannot have escaped observation.
It will now be seen how anxiously he could, with true paternal
solicitude, safeguard the interests of a humble student.  On
one occasion an Overture by Berton was to be performed at
the Institute, together with a Cantata written by one of
Cherubini's pupils.  Berton, resolved to make a noise if
nothing else, applied to Cherubini for the loan of the big
drum, cymbals, and triangles belonging to the Conservatoire, and, no doubt, the master's first impulse was to
consent, as a matter of course.  That impulse he resisted,
however, by extreme thoughtfulness and circumspection,
which led him to address Berton thus:

Will you allow me to make an observation with regard to this
matter?  It is this: I think it out of place to employ these
instruments within the walls of the Institute, especially when

the composition they have to accompany is by an academician. I say nothing of the uproar such a combination will produce, but I may remark that your Overture will crush the Cantata of the poor student who comes afterwards, and his feeble powers will not be able to struggle against it. I defend my pupil, as I would yours under similar circumstances. Thus, my dear Berton, for all these reasons I beg you to give up the notion of having the Overture performed by military instruments. There is no scarcity of beautiful Overtures of your composition, amongst which you might find a preferable one. I think you will feel the force of my argument and kindly appreciate it.

This letter speaks volumes for Cherubini's generous nature. It shows us the master refusing his friend a favour, and running the risk of giving him umbrage, entirely out of consideration for an obscure youth, whose name, even, has not come down to us.

Let us now see what was the conduct of the "grim Florentine" in relation to Lesueur when that composer was timorously making his first essay as a writer for the stage. Happening one day to be at the Théâtre Feydeau when Lesueur was rehearsing his initial opera, the master's attention became attracted by the inexperience and embarassment of the composer, who, unacquainted with stage business, was permitting serious faults to pass uncorrected. For a while Cherubini looked on impatiently, and then, starting up, said, "You can write music, but you do not know how to make them perform it." With these words he took the bâton and conducted the rehearsal to its end, earning in a few minutes Lesueur's everlasting gratitude. After like manner did he behave to Boieldieu, who himself tells a remarkable story of an encounter with Cherubini during the run of " Le Calife de Bagdad " :—

Meeting me in one of the corridors of the theatre, Cherubini seized hold of me by my coat-collar and said, with his somewhat rough frankness, " Unhappy wretch, are you not ashamed to achieve so great a success and do so little to deserve it ? " I remained stupefied at his words—I might well have been so at even less—and could find nothing to say in reply. But after Cherubini had left me, feeling how much reason there was in his reproach, I lost no time in going to him and asking his advice. It was settled that he should take me with him to the country-house of Saint-Just, the writer of my librettos, including the libretto of " Le Calife," and that he should there make me have

an unpleasant time of it. I did so for two seasons. After that
I knew what I was about. But for Cherubini I should probably
still be ignorant that science in no way detracts from expression.

This event was the beginning of a long and intimate
connection between the composers. Cherubini never
abated his interest in Boieldieu's fortunes, and admitted
him to all the privileges of close friendship, even to that
of pointing out faults. It is said of the Italian master
that he rarely met a request with other than a refusal.
This was his habit, and contributed no little to give him
a reputation for unkindness. Strangers took the "No"
as final, and went away calling him a churl. Those,
however, who knew the man asked a second time, and
then the "No" was, more often than otherwise, changed
to "Yes." Boieldieu studied this curious part of his
friend's character to considerable advantage, and could
obtain from him almost anything he wished. But he
could not break Cherubini's habit of saying "No" to a
first application, and one day, patience giving way a little,
he remarked, "Oh! my dear Cherubini, what a pity your
second impulse never precedes your first! It would be so
agreeable for those who have business with you if it did!"

The theorist, Catel, was another who benefited by the
kind heart which throbbed under Cherubini's rough exterior.
He published his famous "Treatise on Harmony" while
still a very young man, but he was not too young for the
great master's notice. Cherubini actually wrote an article
on the book, in which he said:—

It so reconciles them (the different systems of the schools)
with each other that its usefulness and merit cannot be
contested, save by the self-sufficiency of prejudice, by jealousy
or bad faith. Citizen Catel has proved that youth is no obstacle
to the production of what appears beyond its strength, experience, meditation, and natural talent, improved by study,
have brought with them the ripeness of age before the usual
time, and every one who judges men and things impartially
will see in Citizen Catel an artist who will do his country
honour, and in his Treatise a work which will at last be
generally adopted.

What such testimony as this, coming from such a
quarter, was worth to the young musician is easily
imagined. Let us now turn to a remarkable proof of
Cherubini's generosity. Grétry's death, in 1813, vacated

a chair at the Institute, and among the candidates who aspired to fill it was Monsigny, then a man of eighty-five, who had produced nothing for forty years. It was, perhaps, not unnatural that the members of the Institute inclined to prefer Cherubini, a great and active master, to the aged composer whom the world had almost forgotten. At any rate, some of them openly talked of putting up the Florentine as a candidate. Hearing of this, Cherubini wrote a noble letter, saying :—

Not wishing to oppose an artist of M. Monsigny's merit and age, I would beg those members of the fourth class who may intend giving me their suffrages to unite them for the Nestor of French composers, in order that he may be elected as he deserves to be—unanimously.

The master saw his wish gratified, and old Monsigny lived several years to enjoy the distinction he had coveted for half-a-century.

M. Pougin brings forward many other instances of Cherubini's goodness and genuine nobility, but those to which the reader's attention has been directed amply suffice for agreement with the French biographer when he says: —

Cherubini was, therefore, always ready to be useful or agreeable to his colleagues, and constantly employed, either in a quiet manner or before the eyes of the public, in helping them, in assisting them in their career, their efforts, and even the completion of their education. If the abruptness, the *quasi*-brutality for which he was afterwards reproached, and which resulted from his state of health and his continual condition of over nervous excitement, was, indeed, one of the disagreeable elements in his character, we must allow that he amply redeemed the slight drawbacks attached to it by acts so full of generosity and loyalty. Eager to do good, ignorant of what envy or jealousy was, Cherubini was always ready when a service had to be done, and there was perhaps not a single one among his colleagues who had not cause to be grateful to him for something or other, and reason to consider himself lucky in having met him on his path. We know that Spontini, whose admirable genius was seconded only by an education which unfortunately was very incomplete, would, without Cherubini, probably never have mastered the inextricable confusion of the instrumentation in " La Vestale," and we remember the signal service Cherubini did Hummel by making known in Paris the latter's music, which he brought back with him from Vienna."

It is now time to look at Cherubini in his ordinary relations with eminent contemporaries—those who did not need his friendly services, but only desired his friendship. Rossini was one of these, and, when passing through Paris to London in 1823, he did not fail to call upon his illustrious countryman, whom he had never met. The story of their interview has thus been told :—

He (Rossini) went to the residence of Cherubini, and, having been ushered into the drawing-room, sat down at the piano, while waiting for the master of the place, and struck up at the top of his voice—he had a superb one—an air from "Guilio Sabino," one of Cherubini's earliest Italian operas, which Rossini had learnt in his youth from the very artist who created the part. Cherubini came in while he was singing, and said, not without some slight emotion, "Che, che, che, so you know that air, do you ? " "Yes, I do, Maestro, as you perceive." "And where the deuce did you hear it, for it is a very long time since it used to be played ? " "Oh!" replied Rossini, carrying out his graceful compliment, "I heard it in the streets, where it is still sung ; and having a good memory, I have retained it." Cherubini was delighted and they were quickly friends.

When Rossini afterwards settled in Paris these masters formed a close intimacy, though, perhaps, no two men were ever more unlike. Rossini became a frequent visitor at the Florentine's house, and, with characteristic freedom, did not scruple sometimes to take his austere countryman to task. On one occasion he even made bold to interfere in Cherubini's family arrangements. The elder master had a daughter, Zenobia, to whose marriage with an Italian *diplomat* he was strongly adverse. Rossini naturally took the girl's part, and, one day at dinner, urged her father to sanction the union.

"Che, che, che," said Cherubini, "you will kill me if you talk like that." "Confound it," replied Rossini, "you have nothing. You find an idiot ready to take your daughter without a dowry, without an outfit, without anything, and yet you turn up your nose at him. It is absurd." "Che, che, che, I will not allow any one to speak to me in that manner," answered Cherubini, getting angry. "Oh! you will not frighten me," said Rossini, laughing. "You possess more talent than I do, that is well known ; but my *pizzicati* are worth more than all your fugues, look you."

Cherubini tolerated and, in his heart, even enjoyed the

brilliant sallies of his fascinating countryman. Hence the pleasure he always seemed to feel in Rossini's company, and the genuine affection which found vent when "Guillaume Tell" was produced. Cherubini was one of those who attended Habeneck's orchestra from the theatre to Rossini's house for the purpose of serenading him, and he it was who headed a deputation to present the successful composer with a gold wreath. The two men fell into each other's arms and embraced with effusion. That Rossini ardently reciprocated his friend's feeling, a thousand circumstances go to prove, one especially of a date as recent as 1855. In that year the master discovered a portrait of Cherubini in a broker's shop. It represented him as a young man, and was a charming picture, though no one could tell anything about its history. Rossini bought it, of course, and sent a photograph copy to Madame Cherubini, with a note saying :—

Here is the portrait of the great man, who is still as young in your heart as he is in my mind. Kindly accept it as a tender memento from your affectionate G. Rossini.

The portrait thus presented vanished after Madame Cherubini's death and cannot now be found, though M. Pougin believes that some Englishman secured it for a good round sum.

Ferdinand Hiller was another of Cherubini's visitors, and has given to the world a most interesting account of the master as he found him—an acount which may fairly be set against the remarks made on the same subject by Mendelssohn in the days of his youth. Hiller thus describes the Italian master's personal appearance :—

I was somewhat disappointed on entering his study to find a small spare man. But the disappointment was only momentary. There was a penetrating light in his eyes ; tufts of white hair fringed his head, which was comparatively majestic ; and his features, though somewhat impaired by age, still showed traces of almost regular beauty. His general appearance was that of a distinguished statesman rather than a musical composer. This may be seen in the magnificent portrait by Ingres, which seems not so much painted as sculptured in colours, and which reproduces Cherubini's face with wonderful truth.

The German musician then goes on to give a curious confirmation of what has already been said regarding

F

Cherubini's habit of refusing requests and then granting them :—

He was particularly attached to the letter of the law, and his usual reply, " It cannot be done," has become, so to speak, proverbial. At the beginning of our acquaintanceship I had occasion to find, however, that there was a kind heart under this disagreeable form. I had asked leave to take home two volumes from the Conservatoire library, and received an answer " It cannot be done ; it is not allowed." It was useless to press my request, so I changed the conversation ; but as I was bidding him good-bye he said, " What did you want to borrow from our library ? " When I replied that it was a collection of Palestrina's motetts, the old gentleman answered, in an almost confidential tone, " I will send for them for myself. In this manner you can have them." . . One favour which he granted me a few days only before I left Paris, and still more the manner in which it was granted, are too characteristic not to be recorded here. I asked him to give me one of his manuscripts. The last Sunday I spent in Paris he invited me to dine with his family, and before we sat down to table handed me two scores, begging me to choose one of them. Without examining them very attentively I seized on the more bulky of the two, and was about putting it in my pocket, when the well-known " It cannot be done" sounded in my ears. It appears that the manuscripts had their proper place, duly marked according to the letter and number affixed to them, in his library, and that they could not be removed at any price. On the following Tuesday, however, I received a copy of the score I had chosen (a fine "Agnus Dei"), which the indefatigable old gentleman had made in two days, with a trembling hand but with the greatest clearness and neatness. Some letters I afterwards received from him are written in terms of such tender kindness that it is impossible to recognise in them the severe director with his " It cannot be done." I feel certain that he would never have accustomed himself, except in writing, to employ the expressions he used in his letters to me.

Hiller thus sums up the master's character :—

Excellent and honourable in all his actions, and, to the very bottom of his heart, of a kindly and well-nigh naïve nature, his most friendly words and acts were tinged with a kind of bitterness. It was evident that he felt no anxiety as to whether he himself or his music was agreeable. Endowed with clear intelligence and sound judgment, never did he soften the harshness of his remarks by any gentle expression. Like the mild chestnut tree, his very good nature had a rough bark.

How superficially must the young Mendelssohn have judged the master when he said :—

You would never have imagined a man could be a great composer without possessing sensibility, heart, or any other kind of sentiment, whatever its name might be.  Well, I declare to you that with Cherubini everything comes from the brain alone.

With Auber, Cherubini's relations were as intimate as with Rossini.  He had made the brilliant Frenchman's acquaintance when as yet he was "about town," with fine prospects from his father, and only taking up music in an amateurish sort of way for personal amusement.  It was under these circumstances that the two men became familiar, the elder showing towards the younger an almost paternal regard.  Presently Auber's father died without leaving the expected fortune, and the son, gravely perplexed, went to Cherubini for advice.  " The matter is very simple," said the Florentine ; " you are a musician ; you have ideas ; work."  " That is very easily said," replied Auber; " but I am not accustomed to it, and it is not to my taste."  " Very well," was the retort, "then throw yourself out of the window."  This was not to the Frenchman's taste either, and in the end he began taking lessons of his friend—at the age of thirty-five!—with what results all the world knows.  Halévy was another pupil of the great master, and not only a pupil but a familiar friend, for whom there were always an open door and a place at table.  In return, Halévy's love was that of a son.  At Cherubini's funeral he acted as a pall-bearer—"large tears were coursing down his cheeks, and at each roll of the funeral drums, at each plaint of the instruments singing the sublime 'Requiem' which accompanied the great artist's remains, he staggered as though struck to the heart."  We are indebted to Halévy for a fine glimpse of Cherubini's character as it took shape in his last days, when the proud spirit kept old age and death at arm's length till the last moment.  With the subjoined quotation we end our illustrations of the master's personal traits :—

It was on March 15, 1842, that he succumbed, bowed down by years, but struggling courageously against death, as up to that supreme day he had struggled courageously against old age, which had in consequence respected him.  He had preserved all his energy of will, all his distinctness of judgment,

all his clearness of intelligence. . . . He repelled old age out
of pride, the cause of his force and resistance. His clear-
sighted genius kept watch with too much zeal and inquietude
for him not to perceive the enemy's persevering attacks, and not
to feel its cold blows, knowing very well he would be vanquished
the day on which he was not the stronger. Men of this stamp,
who esteem naught in life but intelligence, live on fighting to
the end and die fully armed. "I am beginning to get old!" he
said to me one day. He was then more than eighty. These
words, which would have been commonplace coming from other
lips, struck me grievously proceeding from his, and filled me
with sadness. I saw in them the presentiment and symptom of
approaching dissolution. For me his death began on that day.
Three months later he was no more. His life was, therefore,
exempt from the period of trouble and enfeeblement in which
the faculties are obscured and the gleams of the soul extinguished
—a slow and painful state of transition, during which death is
installed. . . . One might almost fancy that the noble Muse,
whom the brush of Ingres imagined and placed by the composer's
side, sustained him down to the last day with her vigorous hand,
and preserved him from the peril surrounding vulgar lives.

M. Arthur Pougin finishes the chapter devoted to
Cherubini's relations with his contemporaries in these
words: "I will here terminate this long chapter, not because
more documents fail me, but because it threatens to go on
for ever and fatigue the reader." In truth, however, the
reader could stand a great deal more of the same kind, for
here we have a contribution to the master's real biography.
It removes the veil that covers the more personal life of the
man, and enables us to penetrate beneath the conventional
mask which every individual, above all the public individual,
is compelled to wear. Happily, M. Pougin does not omit
reference to Cherubini and Berlioz. In our sketch of the
French composer's life[*] the opinion which Berlioz had formed
regarding the head of the Paris Conservatoire is set forth
by copious extracts from his "Memoirs." It there plainly
appears that Berlioz cherished a genuine animus against
the Italian master, and not only held him up to ridicule—in
itself a sufficient offence, considering the relative positions
of the two men—but tried to make him hateful as well,
crediting him, for example, with mean and despicable
motives. Our readers may possibly remember the case of
the "Requiem" composed by Berlioz, at the instance of

---

* Novello's Primers of Musical Biography. Hector Berlioz.

the Government, for the anniversary of the July Revolution, but actually performed at the Invalides in memory of General Damrémont and the heroes of Constantine. Berlioz tells the world in his " Memoirs" that he chanced to be at the office of the *Journal des Débats* one day when Halévy called to interview the editor, Bertin, and to tell him that the preference of the Government for the French composer had so affected Cherubini as to make him ill. Berlioz adds that :—

Halévy had come to beg M. Bertin to use his power to obtain for the illustrious master the Commander's Cross of the Legion of Honour by way of consolation. M. Bertin's stern voice then interrupted him with these words, " Yes, my dear Halévy, we will do what you wish in order that a distinction he has well merited shall be bestowed upon Cherubini. But as to the ' Requiem,' if any arrangement regarding his work is proposed to Berlioz, and he is weak enough to yield a hair's breadth, I will not speak to him again as long as I live." Halévy must have withdrawn rather more than confounded by this answer.

In reply, M. Pougin does not call Berlioz a liar outright, but he more than insinuates as much. Here are his words :—

I do not hesitate to declare that Berlioz here lost a fine occasion of holding his tongue, and that this little narrative does more honour to his invention than to his delicacy. What person will he make believe that Cherubini, of whom we cannot cite a single trait of envy or jealousy in the whole course of his career, was so jealous of Berlioz as to be " ill in bed " in consequence ? . . . What person will he make believe that Cherubini could commission any one to go to M. Bertin and beg a Commander's collar of the Legion of Honour for him, a Member of the Institute, the Director of the Conservatory, an artist illustrious among the most illustrious, and who certainly needed no one's "patronage " or "recommendation" to obtain no matter what? What person, lastly, will he make believe that, desiring so eagerly this distinction, Cherubini had to wait for it several years, since he did not receive it till 1844, towards the end of his life, when he resigned the post which he held in the Conservatory? Of a truth, all this is puerile, as well as rather naïve, and calculated to prove that Berlioz was merely a persistent hater.

The foregoing argument to character first appeared in *Le Ménestrel*—M. Pougin's work being published by weekly instalments—and at once drew remonstrance and complaint from the admirers of Berlioz. M. Pougin lost no time in putting forth a crushing reply, beginning thus : " I am absolutely obliged to remark to my kind correspondents that my severity was, if anything, rather less than it should have been." He then went on to observe that Berlioz had actually written to Cherubini on the very matter in question, thanking him for efforts made on behalf of himself and his " Requiem." Here is the conclusive document :—

Sir—I am deeply touched by the noble abnegation which has led you to refuse your admirable " Requiem " for the ceremony at the Invalides. Kindly believe that I am profoundly grateful. As, however, the determination of the Minister of the Interior is irrevocable, I now earnestly beg you to think no longer of me, and not to deprive the Government and your admirers of a master-piece which would throw so much lustre on the solemnity. I remain, with profound respect, Sir, your devoted servant, H. Berlioz.

Although some points in this letter are not quite clear, it leaves no doubt of the main fact at issue, and compels us to agree with M. Pougin when he says of Berlioz that he " did not always trouble himself to observe the exact truth with regard to things on which he was better informed than any one else."

Cherubini's record, between his appointment as Master of the Royal Chapel, in 1814, and as Director of the Con-servatoire, in 1822, is almost entirely taken up with compositions for the Church. His secular works during that period are easily enumerated. Thus we read of a Cantata, " Le Mariage de Salomon," written for the wedding festivities of the Duc de Berri, and performed at the Tuileries, June 17, 1816. This was shortly.followed by a two-voice romance, " Je ne t'aime plus," two pieces for oboe and bassoon respectively, and an air for " Lodoiska," in view of a revival of that opera. In 1821, the birth of a son (the late Count de Chambord) to the Duchesse de Berri caused Cherubini to write a " Cantata for several voices, with choruses interspersed," which was performed at the Hôtel de Ville, on May 2. He also collaborated with Berton, Boieldieu, Kreutzer, and Paer in the production of a one-act Opera, " Blanche de Provence," first represented at the Court Theatre, on May 1, and subsequently twice at the Académie Royale, then located in the Théâtre Favart, the opera house having been destroyed after the Duc de Berri's assassination. M. Pougin says :—

Of this unfortunate work all that survived was an adorable

chorus of the most exquisite effect, " Dors, mon enfant," which formed part of the third tableau, precisely the one written by Cherubini. This chorus, still celebrated, was inscribed in the programme of the first Concert given on March 9, 1828, by the Société des Concerts du Conservatoire; since then it has always remained in the repertory of that famous institution.

It was of this chorus, no doubt, that Moscheles, who attended a performance, wrote in his diary: " The final chorus, by Cherubini, made an indelible impression on my mind."

The more important sacred works during this period were an "Iste Dies" (1817), a "Tantum ergo" (1817), a " Regina Cœli " (1818), of which a French critic, Girod, remarks :— " It is incontestably the most beautiful piece of its kind, and a magnificent ovation to the Queen of Heaven "; and a Mass in E, attributable to the last-named year, but, according to one authority, not yet published. To 1819 belongs the Mass in G, composed for the coronation of Louis XVIII. This, it should be observed, is not the work generally known as Cherubini's " Coronation Mass," which was written five years later for the ceremony wherein Charles X. acted the principal part. The Mass of 1819 brought Cherubini at least an honorary recompense. He was created a Knight of the Order of St. Michael— one of those ephemeral distinctions which sprang up with the return of the Bourbons, only to be crushed by the next revolution. To the year just named belongs also the Quartet in E flat, which, if Spohr's evidence may be credited, was composed in ignorance of the masterpieces by Mozart and Beethoven. From evidence supplied by M. Pougin, it would appear that, about this time, Cherubini much desired the managership of the Opera, and was actually a candidate for the place against his old friend Viotti, who carried off the honour. This seems to have been unknown, or, at any rate, unremembered, till M. Pougin found, among the documents entrusted to him by Cherubini's family, a letter from Viotti (dated November 5, 1819), after his appointment. In that letter, Viotti said :—

I have been informed, my dear friend, that you are angry. If it is with me, you are wrong, and it will not be difficult for me to convince you of this. . . I did not seek the post with which I am honoured or the position which once more puts an end to my tranquillity. The whole matter has been arranged I know not how, and it was only ten days or a fortnight ago that I was sent for from Châtillon to give my consent. . . As a matter of course I appreciate profoundly the kindness of the Comte de Pradel ; he has a right to my gratitude and I shall do all I can to prove this to him ; but I cannot help feeling extremely sorry at having been the rival of a friend whom I love and whose genius I have always respected and appreciated—of a man whom I shall never cease to love, whatever change may take place in his heart.

A letter thus frank and manly should have soothed Cherubini's ruffled spirit, at least as regards the writer ; but this does not appear to have been the case, and the two friends were never again to each other quite as before.

We now come to the time (1822) when Cherubini found himself at the head of the great institution which he, as a professor, had helped to establish.

On April 19, 1822, the Minister of the King's Household formally invested our master with all the honours and privileges of Director of the Royal School of Music for a term of twenty years, *vice* Perne resigned. The choice took nobody by surprise, for not only was Cherubini the greatest available composer, but the most successful professor. With three of his pupils he had, in five years, won seven nominations to the Grand Prix de Rome. All circumstances, therefore, pointed out Cherubini as a man likely to raise the school from the depths into which it had fallen since the Restoration, and he soon began to justify the trust reposed in him. M. Pougin thus sums up the comprehensive measures carried out under the *régime* of the new director :—

Not only was his directorship fertile in salutary measures and ameliorations of every kind, but it was specially excellent as regards the exactitude, the method, and the regularity in the work of each day, the general course of study, and the happy impulse imparted to every branch of instruction. It was under Cherubini's reign that a double committee of instruction was created for music and for elocution, as well as a committee of management ; that the boarding-house for male pupils (and even that for female pupils, which it was afterwards necessary to do away with) was re-opened ; that public performances were re-established and their number fixed ; that the terms of engagement between the pupils and the Theatres Royal were settled ; that classes for the harp, double-bass, preparatory piano for women, and reading aloud were created ; that opera and comic opera and instruction in lyrical declamation were divided into two distinct branches ; that the schools of music in the departmental towns of Lille, Toulouse, Marseilles, and Metz were created branches of the parent school ; that the terms on which the professors should retire were exactly defined, &c.

This statement says enough for Cherubini as an organiser and administrator—as, in fact, a man of business in his art. It would be easy to add many other particulars, such as those found, for example, in Lassabathie's *Histoire du Conservatoire*. There we learn that the master devoted his whole time to the work of the institution. His discipline was severe and carried out under his own personal observation, as, by the way, Berlioz found when he presumed to enter the Conservatoire building by the door set apart for female students. As he was himself, so he expected all the professors and servants to be. Ever firm and impartial, he gave way to no considerations but those of strict duty. He even dared to refuse the request of royalty. On one occasion Queen Marie-Amélie recommended a certain Mdlle. Hebler for admission into the school, little doubting but that, as usual in such cases, her request would be acted upon as a command. Cherubini answered her Majesty's private secretary thus :—

I have just heard Mdlle. Hebler, whom you did me the honour to recommend on the part of the queen, and who desired to be admitted into the Conservatoire. Despite all my inclination to second her majesty's kind intentions with regard to the young lady, I regret very much that it is impossible for me to receive her, on account of the feebleness of her natural means. I acquainted her verbally with the motives preventing her admission, and advised her mother to bring her up to some other career than that of the stage, for which nature has denied her the most indispensable qualities—exterior and voice.

Cherubini could say " No " to his best friends with equal readiness, when duty seemed to require it. We are told that, on one occasion, Halévy used his influence on behalf of a lady, well endowed with musical means, whose husband had suffered a heavy reverse of fortune. The Director's favourite pupil simply requested that she might be admitted to Levasseur's operatic class, with a view to earning a living on the stage. Cherubini readily consented to an interview with the applicant, and when she entered the room, said : " Are you the lady, madam, who wished to come out at the opera ? " " Yes, sir." " It is impossible." " Why, sir ? "

"Why! Ask your glass." We agree with M. Pougin's comment upon this: "It was harsh, without doubt, and somewhat brutal, but was it not artistically honest?" The qualities of harshness and roughness to which reference is here made, and has often been made before, seem to have developed under the constant friction of a great institution, with its conflicting interests and many worries. This was partly the result of over-zeal. Cherubini would insist on seeing to everything himself, and taking directly upon his own shoulders responsibilities which should have been left to subordinates. Yet the entire Conservatoire felt the influence of his untiring and unswerving honesty. His influence descended through all grades to the lowest, and the great French School rapidly became great in the best sense of the term.

Many stories are told of Cherubini's punctilious regard for what most people look upon as small matters. On one occasion he said to the Minister of the King's Household, who was behind time at a prize distribution, "You are very late, Monseigneur!" Habeneck, it appears, would never learn punctuality, and was always being rated in consequence. One day, however, he bustled in hot with hurry and said triumphantly to the Director, "You cannot reproach me now!" Cherubini looked at his watch and answered, "You are three minutes too soon; you are not punctual now." As regards the Director's very plain speaking, the following stories are not without interest :—

At an examination of condidates for admission as singing pupils, a poor misshapen fellow apppeared and sang with excellent taste, displaying also a beautiful voice. The examiners felt that they could not admit a person so disqualified by nature for stage work, but they desired to make known admiration of his talent. Cherubini undertook to settle the matter with the candidate, and going to him said :—

"My young friend, your voice is magnificent. Yes, your voice is superb, and you sing with a great deal of taste. The Committee are, in consequence, delighted to have heard you. At the same time they regret exceedingly they cannot admit you." "What is their reason, sir?" asked the anxious applicant. "What is their reason!" replied Cherubini. "Why, my young friend, because we cannot on your account open a theatre for monkeys."

This, most people will agree with us, was simple brutality,

so unmanly that had the candidate inflicted personal chas-
tisement upon the Director then and there no more than
justice would have been done.

A second story affords more pleasant reading. Miel is
responsible for it, and we may use a translation of his words,
premising that the people concerned were, besides Cherubini,
an anxious father of gigantic stature, and a pretty little boy,
his son, who, being musically gifted, was a candidate for
admission to the Conservatoire.

Advised by their friends, the applicants (tall father and tiny
child) posted themselves in a room which the Director never failed
to traverse when starting on his visit to the class-rooms. On
opening the door, Cherubini found himself confronted by a
colossus, who, from the eminence of his six feet, was awkwardly
holding by the hand a perfect little cherub. Surprised at the
meeting, and, no doubt, taken aback at this contrast between the
extremes of human stature, he said in a haughty tone to the
giant, " What can I do for you ? " Then, on being informed of
his visitor's wish, he added, proceeding on his way, " I do not
take infants to wet nurse." The poor father was thunderstruck.

Subsequently Cherubini found the little boy in one of the
class-rooms, seated at a pianoforte.

There was now no father present. . . . The choice of the
pieces and the manner of their execution struck him ; he stopped,
sat down, and listened. The age, the grace, and the talent of the
executant had produced their effect. Caresses and words of
encouragement were followed by questions ; on the principles of
the art the child was not to be shaken. " Bravo, my little friend ! "
said Cherubini, delighted, "but why are you here, and what can I
do for you?" " Something very easy for you," replied the applicant, "and something which will make me very happy ; admit me
to the Conservatoire." " The thing is *done*," replied the Director,
"you are one of us." Thereupon he left the room and gaily related
what had happened, adding, laughingly, " I took very good care
not to push my questions further, for the brat would have proved
to me that he knew more than I did."

The foregoing tale, which no biographer of Cherubini ven-
tures to omit, is the best practical illustration of Adolphe
Adam's remarks upon his master's character :—

The sensations experienced in approaching Cherubini were
so strange that it would be hard to define them and much more
to understand them. The veneration that you had for his great
age and fine talent, was suddenly altered by ridicule aroused by

little trifles to which he clung with a persevering obstinacy. Then, at the end of a few minutes, as though he had understood that it was too long a time to act the disagreeable to no purpose, his face relaxed, that smile, so refined and shrewd, came to animate the fine head of the old man, good nature resumed the ascendant, little by little the faults of a spoilt child disappeared, he became a good man in spite of himself; his heart opened out to yours, and then you could resist him no more; you left him charmed, and altogether surprised to have felt towards this extraordinary man, in so short a time, sentiments so different—repulsion, admiration, and enthusiasm.

After what has been said regarding the bearing and conduct of Cherubini, there is no need for further details in explanation of his somewhat tyrannical and often stormy reign at the Conservatoire. The master suffered from nerves and gave way to them; his attention to trifles was a perennial source of irritation, and as years went on his sensitiveness grew into a chronic infirmity of temper, so as almost to hide the real goodness that existed beneath. How lovable he was, *au fond*, his pupils have told us with all the warmth of passionate affection.

Cherubini's rule of the Conservatoire was distinguished by the establishment (in 1822) of the famous and still existing Concerts, initiated by Habeneck and supported by the Director with all possible energy. It was through Cherubini that the proposal to give Concerts in the hall of the Conservatoire obtained Government sanction and aid, while the master himself acted as President of the Committee by whom the new institution was managed. It is important to observe that the main purpose was the performance of Beethoven's works. Both English and Germans are apt to sneer at the backwardness of the French as regards appreciation of Beethoven, but we may reasonably question whether any society outside France can show such a record of true homage to that master as the Société des Concerts du Conservatoire. Mr. Bellasis tells us that in thirty-four years there were 280 performances of his symphonies, 38 of his overtures, 41 of his works for the chamber; in all, 359. As for the great "Choral" Symphony, till within the last few years almost unknown in England, it was executed in Paris during the above-mentioned period no fewer than nineteen times. The wonderful perfection of the concerts given under Habeneck has often been described, and the secret of it is found, as usual, in the absolute authority of one master mind, having at command unlimited opportunities for impressing upon subordinates his slightest will. We have now amongst us an eminent artist—M. Sainton—who belonged to Habeneck's orchestra, and can tell of the extraordinary preparation which that body had to undergo. Every section was separately rehearsed again and again, if needful, till all its component parts worked together like one man ; the first violins, for example, bowing every passage with absolute uniformity, and playing with such regulated expression—the expression determined by the conductor—that the effect might have come from a single instrument. The sections being thus drilled, the grand divisions were brought together, and finally the entire orchestra, so that, in performance, each player was but a machine carrying out his part of a great executive design conceived by the one presiding mind. It is thus, and only thus, that famous things are done in the performance of musical masterpieces. Compared with the result so produced, that attained by English orchestras after, at best, two rehearsals, is but a scramble, wherein whatever appears really excellent comes from chance, or the power of extraordinary skill triumphing over adverse conditions.

Another memorable incident of Cherubini's period at the Conservatoire is the publication (1835) of his " Cours de Contrepoint et de Fugue," in order that, as he himself said:—

Instruction in counterpoint should form part of the course of study in the establishment which I have the honour of directing—

words that mean, perhaps, more attention to counterpoint, rather than the setting it up as a new study. The Director seems to have intended presenting this work to the Académie, and a memorandum intended to accompany it was found among his papers. This document begins by declaring that counterpoint is universal rather than national—" the same in all countries." It then continues :—

By counterpoint the faculty of composing purely and vigorously is acquired. Thus, when a man is thoroughly master of counterpoint and fugue, he is certain of being an accomplished composer ; he then knows sufficient to give himself up to the impulses of genius and imagination, to undertake what is called high composition, whether vocal or instrumental. It is then that the Italian, German, or French style may be embraced, according to the choice, taste, and liking of a young composer. But he must, above all, have learned counterpoint, as mentioned above.

It is not quite needless to cite these remarks at the present moment.

It is now time to speak of the compositions which Cherubini gave to the world in his last years—that is to say, between 1830, when the choir of the Chapel Royal and his office connected therewith were suppressed, and 1839, when he ceased to write. During that period, the master, as may be supposed, was several times tempted to resume work in connection with the lyric stage. M. Pixérécourt, author of the drama, " Les Mines de Pologne," from which the libretto of " Faniska" was taken, had previously sought Cherubini's help in an adaptation of the work for the Opéra Comique. The composer consented, but found, on looking at the score, that it could not be made to suit a French audience, and the project consequently fell through. Indeed his zeal for opera had abated, in presence of increasing love for the music of the Church. It was, therefore, with no great hope of success that Scribe and Mélesville approached him on the subject of his opera, " Koukourgi," written in 1793, and never produced. M. Pougin gives a very clear account of the transaction that ensued, and his words may be quoted with advantage :—

Why was the work never brought out ? That is what no one to-day can tell. One thing, however, is certain : the libretto was supplied by Duveyrièr, father of the ingenious and fertile dramatic author who made himself known under the name of Mélesville, and who, wishing to derive some profit from the paternal prose, suggested to Scribe, his usual literary colleague, the idea of joining him in re-arranging the book of " Koukourgi," which no longer suited the taste of the day, and of making the public acquainted with Cherubini's music. The two authors called upon the composer, and explained to him their desire, which he seems to have agreed to without much pressure. As is invariably the case under such circumstances, they were to follow almost exactly the original course of the story, so that the situations might be reproduced, and the sense of the music and the form of the numbers not changed. But, as is also invariably the case, changes and modifications cropped up in the course of the work, and the musician was bound to have his share of them. Thus Cherubini was obliged to write a large number of new pieces. Then " Koukourgi " was in three acts only, while " Ali Baba "—such were the new title and subject adopted—was in four, with a prologue ; moreover, the work was remodelled, and first destined for the Opéra Comique, was eventually taken to the Opéra, and naturally subjected to fresh modifications and important alterations. It was not, consequently, till after the lapse of several years that it could possibly be brought out.

Fétis states that the work thus laboriously put together was "almost entirely new," and that the manuscript ran to no less than a thousand pages. He adds, with great truth and force :—

It is something marvellous that a master whose first compositions are dated 1773 should have been able to write with the spirit of youth, sixty years afterwards, an immense musical work; modify his talent with rare facility, without ceasing to be himself; find fresh and brilliant ideas, when only experience and learning were expected from him, and light upon accents of love and passion in a septuagenarian heart.

We have seen that the work was carried to the Opéra, but it must not be supposed that the authorities of the grand theatre were very anxious to have it. Dr. Véron, the then director, accepted "Ali Babi" against his own judgment, entirely out of respect for an illustrious old composer. Nor does it appear that Cherubini himself cherished very sanguine hopes. We learn from Halévy that, though he attended the rehearsals—and at times made his presence very much felt there—he ran away from the performance, going to Versailles, and, watch in hand, letting his fancy follow what was at the moment being done in Paris. "At five-and-twenty minutes past eleven 'Ali Baba' was over by his watch, which, he said, went very well and kept Opéra time." He retired to bed, slept soundly, returned to Paris only after having received a re-assuring despatch, and never went to see this opera, of which he never spoke again, except to observe, "It is too old to live long. It was forty when it came into the world." Readers of the Memoirs of Berlioz may remember that, according to his own account, that excellent hater of Cherubini greatly distinguished himself by offering an increasing number of francs for an idea, and it must be said in some sort of justification that the Parisians generally had no great opinion of "Ali Baba." It was played four times, set aside for two months while Nourrit took his holidays, reproduced on that artist's return, and soon finally withdrawn. Mr. Bellasis quotes from

Boigne's " Petits Memoires de l'Opéra " a rather amusing account of its first night's reception :—

In " Ali Baba " everything was wearisome and soporific— poem, music, and ballet ; the airs of which were, however, composed by Halévy.   Those fastidious forty thieves had better have rested eternally in their jars and in the works of Galland. Cherubini demanding hospitality at the Opéra for " Ali Baba " has the same effect with me as would Belisarius holding out his helmet to the passers by.   " Ali Baba " is one of those fossilised operas which a director only accepts when they are thrust down his throat by illustrious old age, and for fear of being declared a vandal, the director had to pass it off for a *chef d'œuvre*, and with a loss of fifty to sixty thousand francs.   But the public, who were not bound by the same considerations as M. Véron, yawned so much and so widely, under *Ali Baba's* very nose, that real hissing would have spoken less eloquently.   The public condemned without appeal, and executed pitilessly those forty thieves who had not stolen anything.

The same writer tells us—we may acccept the statement or not—that Cherubini laid all the blame of failure on the chorus, remarking, " With such miserable choristers as those of the Opéra no success is possible.   I could never make one of my forty thieves sing, or even march, in time." Mendelssohn, as readers of his letters may recollect, criticised the music of the piece with his usual freedom, declaring that, though " enchanted " with many parts, he could not accept Cherubini's new-fangled orchestration, in which it seemed "as if the instruments were nothing and the effect everything. . . . As if it were the audience who had skins of parchment instead of the drums."   On the other hand, a writer in the *Niederrheinische Musik Zeitung* said :—

Cherubini was seventy-three years of age, but both his head and his heart had remained young, and his latest dramatic production displayed, in conjunction with the maturest knowledge and the most beautiful form, the loveliest blossoms of profound feeling and youthful passion.   That the work did not retain its place in the repertory was not astonishing in the case of a public intoxicated by the perfumes arising from the flowery path which Rossini and his imitators had forced the opera to take.

This was not the only remark of German appreciation. " Ali Baba," produced in Paris, July 22, 1833, was performed in Berlin, February 27, 1835, " with great success." Thenceforth the old master wrote no more for the stage.

It has been stated on an earlier page that Cherubini diversified his labours, when about fifty years of age, by writing a string Quartet in E flat. We now find him, nearly a quarter of a century later, returning with almost youthful zest to that form of composition ; which, no doubt, he found better suited to his years than the more exciting labour of operas and masses. "It occupies and amuses me," he said to Ferdinand Hiller, "for I have not the least pretension in the matter." About the value of this music connoisseurs differ greatly. For example, Professor Macfarren, having before him the Quartet in E flat (1814) and that in C (1829), founded on Cherubini's London Symphony, writes in the " Imperial Dictionary " as follows :—

Their merit entitles them to no distinction, and it is scarcely to be supposed that his several subsequent works of the same class which have not been printed can possess any greater interest, since these prove the author's entire want of feeling for the style, and aptitude for the form, of instrumental chamber.music.

On the other hand, Hiller describes the Quartet as "full of delicacy and piquancy," which indeed it is ; Schumann speaks of it as "full of life," and adds that the Finale sparkles "like a diamond when you shake it"; while Fétis remarks of all the Quartets:—

These compositions are of a very high order. Cherubini has here a style of his own, as in all his works. He imitates neither the manner of Haydn, nor that of Mozart, nor that of Beethoven.

Between Professor Macfarren and the majority opposed to him, we shall not pretend to decide; but simply express a modest opinion that Cherubini's instrumental works for the chamber are not only interesting—as, bearing his name, they must needs be—but a distinct and valuable addition to the repertory of their class, because so full of fresh and charming individuality. The revival of the old master's regard for this form of music seems to have been due to the eminent violinist, Baillot, who introduced the Quartet in E flat at one of his Quartet parties with much applause. Then, as we have seen, Cherubini founded a second upon the symphony written in London, and subsequently composed four others, three of which, it appears, still remain in manuscript. Concerning the Quartet in C, Schumann says :—

A few dry bars, the work of the intellect alone, there are, as in most of Cherubini's works, but even in these there is always

G

something interesting in the passage, some ingenious con-
trivance or imitation, something to think about.   There is most
spirit in the Scherzo and last movement, which are both full of
wonderful life.   The Adagio has a striking individual A minor
character, something romantic and Provençalish.   After hearing
it several times its charms grow, and it closes in such a manner
as to make you begin listening again, though knowing that the
end is near at hand.

The master's last chamber composition was a Quintet,
written in 1836.   Of this Ferdinand Hiller tells us :—

When I left Paris in 1836, Cherubini was writing a Quintet
for stringed instruments, and told me with perfect simplicity that
he intended to write half-a-dozen more. . . . The Quintet
was executed in his own room, when he was seventy-eight, and
greatly surprised the artists of Paris.

Fétis adds to this :—

In the winter of 1838, Cherubini invited to his house a few
artists, and had performed for them the Quintet he had just
finished.   They all experienced the liveliest emotion at the
work, the author of which was then seventy-eight years old.
Even if we grant that this great age was not entirely without
influence on the impression produced, it is no less true that
every one perceived in the work a freshness of ideas which, it
might have been thought, could scarcely belong to an old man
on the brink of the grave.   Cherubini's hand trembled when
tracing these last emanations of his talent, but his mind had
preserved all its clearness and all its vigour.

Following the Quintet came a few solfeggi, and when
Cherubini, in 1839, had written an arietta for an album, the
old man's work was done ; the pen dropped for ever from his
tired fingers, and the few years of life remaining belonged to
his family and friends alone.   Respectful interest and
admiration naturally desire to follow him into his home, and
happily we are not left to imagine what sort of a place it was,
and how its master bore himself amid relatives and friends.
It need not be pointed out, after what has already been said
as to Cherubini's personal character, that he was no surly
misanthrope, shutting himself up and growling like a bear in
his den.   On the contrary, "the grim Florentine" never
pulled his latch-string in against artists, colleagues, and
friends.   However apparently stern and unsympathetic in
his official relations, at home and in the social circle he was

genial and even gay. Under his roof, if we may believe M. Pougin—

There prevailed an affectionate neighbourly feeling, a charming familiarity, and an intercourse entirely free from restraint, revealing a new and unknown Cherubini—a Cherubini who had lost all his ruggedness ; smiling because he had thrown off the last trace of his official positions ; attentive to every one, and ready to enter into friendly conversation—in a word, quite another Cherubini to the one we have always been shown up to the present time, and very different to the by no means flattering portrait biographers have been pleased to draw of him.

How many distinguished artists used to visit the old man thus revealed to us as happy and lovable in his home ! At times might have been met there Boieldieu and his wife ; Carafa, Berton, Bordogni, the singing-master, and his wife ; Madame Rigault ; Narderman, the harpist; Zimmermann, the pianist ; Viotti, Kalkbrenner, Heller, Chopin, Thalberg, Rossini, and a host of others. These—Viotti excepted, for Cherubini could never forget the affair of the Opéra direction —were admitted into the inner circle, and made free of the house. Most welcome of all, perhaps, to the quiet self-contained Cherubini was boisterous expansive Rossini—*les extrèmes se touchent.*

He who brought with him life, movement, and gaiety; he whose beaming and sonorous laugh, and meridional fluency of speech, together with his vibrating and re-echoing voice, came to disturb with a sort of violence the ordinarily discreet echoes of the always calm and half-silent household was Rossini—Rossini, then in all the prime of age and health, jocose by nature and by taste ; an inexhaustible narrator of good stories, never at a loss for anecdotes and piquant tales ; a man who appeared unable to look at anything seriously ; who had always a bit of sly malice to slip into the conversation, and whom two men only, Cherubini and Boieldieu, could induce to speak of art in a reasonable manner, and without laughing at people.

This great, full life must indeed have come into the house like a whirlwind, making everything whirl and dance in rhythm with itself. When Rossini entered at the door, quietness flew out at the window. " Tranquillity was impossible. He set every one off with his good-humoured sarcasm and rollicking high spirits ! " But when Rossini was not there, order prevailed.

The ladies talked among themselves. Sometimes the com-

pany played at cards : bouillot, all-fours, or whist, Cherubini
willingly taking a hand, especially at whist, of which he was
particularly fond ; sometimes, also, he would play backgammon,
either with Salvador or Gide. On other occasions, when
Boieldieu and Cicéri were there, he would join them. All three
then began drawing, and all three being very clever, produced
some charming things. Sometimes, again, it happened that
Cherubini, leaving his wife to look after his guests, would retire
a little to work. He used to seat himself at the table placed
against his old Erard piano, and there, with a quantity of music
paper under his hand, absorbed and abstracted in his inspiration,
he would write a piece of music without a single erasure or
correction, and afterwards carefully put it away in one of his
portfolios. It mattered nothing to him that twenty persons went
on talking, laughing, and arguing ; provided they did not sing,
it was immaterial to him what they did.

Into this haven of rest and enjoyment Cherubini retired,
when his work in the world was done, and there he awaited
the angel of Death. He was prepared for the coming of the
good spirit, which Gothic fancy has so horribly misrepresented in more than one way. He had, for example, got
ready his own " Requiem," under the circumstances already
detailed. The old master did not keep this work by him, as
sacred to the purpose for which he primarily intended it.
According to Mr. Bellasis, the " Dies Iræ " was performed
at a Conservatoire concert, in March, 1837, and, a year later,
the whole Mass was given under the same auspices.
Previously to this Mendelssohn had heard of it, with perfect
faith in its worth, for we find him writing to the directors of
the Lower Rhine Festival, in January 1838, as thus :—

With regard to the second day, I may first enquire whether
you intend to apply to Cherubini for his grand " Requiem " ; it
must be translated (?) and is entirely for men's voices ; but as it
will only last an hour, even less, that would not much matter,
and, according to the universal verdict, it is a splendid work.

The events of Cherubini's life between the composition of
the Quintet—in effect his last work—and the day when he
passed away, were naturally few. Moscheles tells of a visit
to him in 1839, and of the aged composer saying that :—

With the exception of the Directorship at the Conservatoire,
he had nothing more to do with music ; he couldn't write another
note ; he wasn't strong enough to hear and enjoy musical
impressions.

In 1841 Cherubini sat for his portrait to Ingres, and the result was the well-known picture, half literal, half allegorical, wherein the master appears in his ordinary dress, while Polyhymnia, in classic attire, stretches her hand over her votary. In February, 1842, the old man voluntarily put an end to his long connection with the great school he had helped to found in the stormy days of the Revolution. Failing health made it impossible for him to discharge the duties of his high office, and so strict a disciplinarian was not likely to sanction in himself, for whatever reason, the neglect he had never allowed in others. So he sent in his resignation and insisted on its acceptance, refusing point-blank to avail himself of " unlimited leave of absence." On this, King Louis Philippe, never very ready at generous and graceful acts, woke up to a perception of what was fitting, and bestowed upon Cherubini the Commander's Cross of the Legion of Honour—a dignity never before awarded to a musician. The master enjoyed it but a little while. He rapidly became weaker, and on March 12, 1842, while his family and friends, among whom was the faithful Halévy, stood around his bed, he peacefully fell asleep, in the eighty-second year of his age.

Cherubini's death, though naturally looked for, made a profound impression in musical Europe. The master had lived so long and filled so great a place, that he was instinctively regarded almost as an institution. His departure created a void that nothing seemed able to fill, and from all quarters came the tribute of grief and respectful sympathy. In one English journal it was said :—

Cherubini is no more ! The founder of the French Conservatoire, the instructor of a thousand eminent musicians, the composer of innumerable undying productions, who for more than forty years has been loved by those who knew him personally, and admired by all Europe, who has outlived all rivals, and sustained the highest undisputed glory of his art.

Another English writer compared the master's death to—

The extinguishment of the sacred fire upon an altar, which overspreads the whole temple with a sudden gloom, and leaves but the sweet odour of the incense, which shall burn no more.

After saying that it would be idle grief to lament for one who lived so long and nobly, the same writer went on :—

Still, one cannot help an emotion almost amounting to awe, when we learn that such a man has passed away from among us ; when we are brought to contemplate the rational miracle of a human mind which, for more than seventy years, has continually poured forth its beautiful imaginings in countless variety. When we but surmise how rich and vast the reminiscences and associations of such a mind must be, mingling as it has done with all the brightest and best of its kindred nature during three-quarters of a century ; and when we are forced to know that such a man and such a mind, and such a treasury of golden tokens, are henceforth to be themselves but a memory.

On the other side of the Channel the deceased composer's pupil, Adolphe Adam, lifted up an eloquent voice and said :—

That name shall be immortal, that glory will not perish, for, though Cherubini may cease to be numbered among the first of composers, where is the master who has produced such scholars ? The excellence of his system is best proved by the diversity of talent developed in those who have enjoyed the advantage of his admirable lessons. To each he gave an individuality, but to all that unaffected purity of style of which his own works furnish such beautiful examples, and which it is delightful to see reflected in the compositions of the musical generation he has created.

Cherubini's funeral was worthy of so great a man. The body, after lying in state in the great hall of the Conservatoire, was escorted to the Church of St. Roch by a procession of over three thousand persons in some way or other connected with the musical art. The cortége was preceded by two regiments of infantry in compliment to the rank of the deceased as a Commander of the Legion, a band of sixty-five instruments playing the Dead March written by him for the funeral of General Hoche, and the pall being borne by Auber, Halévy, Ingres, and Raoul-Rochette. In the church the " Requiem " for male voices was performed by the artists of the Opéra, the Italian Opera, and the Opéra Comique, and, at its conclusion, the honoured remains were carried to Père la Chaise. The grave was dug near those of Grétry and Boieldieu, and standing above it Raoul-Rochette, Lafont, Halévy, and a pupil of the Conservatoire eulogised the deceased and bade him farewell, a great crowd listening unaffected by a downpour of hail. So, with fitting rites, passed from the world a great and remarkable man, whose fame will outlive all changes of taste, because the principles his works exemplify are the eternal principles of true art.

# INDEX.

"ABENCÉRAGES, LES" .. .. .. .. ..
"ACHILLE À SEYROS" .. .. .. .. ..
"ADRIANO IN SYRIO" .. .. .. .. ..
"ALESSANDRO NELL' INDIE, L'" .. .. ..
"ALI BABA" .. .. .. .. .. ..
"AMPHION" .. .. .. .. .. ..
"ANACRÉON" .. .. .. .. .. ..
ANECDOTES of CHERUBINI .. .. .. ..
"ARMIDA" .. .. .. .. .. ..
AUBER and CHERUBINI .. .. .. .. ..

BARTOLOMEO CHERUBINI .. .. .. ..
"BAYARD Á MÉZIÈRES" .. .. .. .. ..
BERLIOZ and CHERUBINI .. .. .. ..
BIZARRI, PIETRO .. .. .. .. .. ..
"BLANCHE DE PROVENCE" .. .. .. ..
BOIELDIEU .. .. .. .. .. ..
BOUILLY .. .. .. .. .. .. ..
BRULL, Count von .. .. .. .. ..

CASTRUCCI, GIUSEPPE .. .. .. .. ..
CHERUBINI.. .. .. .. .. .. ..
"CIRCÉ" .. .. .. .. .. .. ..
CONSERVATOIRE, ORIGIN of the .. .. ..
       „       CONCERTS, The .. .. ..
"CORONATION MASS" .. .. .. .. ..
COWPER, Lord .. .. .. .. .. ..
"CRESCENDO, LE" .. .. .. .. ..
CHERUBINI'S parents and family .. .. ..
       „       childhood .. .. .. .. ..
       „       early musical studies .. .. ..
       „        „    compositions .. .. ..
       „       life in Florence .. .. .. ..
       „       first start in life .. .. .. ..
       „       studies under Sarti .. .. ..
       „       first opera .. .. .. .. ..

| | | PAGE |
|---|---|---|
| CHERUBINI'S | operatic labours, 1781-3 .. .. .. .. .. | 9, 10 |
| ,, | visit to England .. .. .. .. .. .. .. | 10 |
| ,, | reception in London .. .. .. .. .. | 10, 11 |
| ,, | visit to Paris .. .. .. .. .. .. .. | 11 |
| ,, | first appearance there .. .. .. .. .. .. | 12 |
| ,, | return to London.. .. .. .. .. .. .. | 13 |
| ,, | re-appearance in Paris .. .. .. .. .. .. | 13 |
| ,, | visit to Turin .. .. .. .. .. .. .. | 14 |
| ,, | success with " Iphigenia " .. .. .. .. .. | 15 |
| ,, | return to Paris .. .. .. .. .. .. .. | 15 |
| ,, | " Demophon " .. .. .. .. .. .. | 17—19 |
| ,, | appointment to the Theatre de Monsieur .. .. .. | 20 |
| ,, | disasters during the Revolution .. .. .. .. | 22 |
| ,, | marriage .. .. .. .. .. .. .. .. | 24 |
| ,, | children .. .. .. .. .. .. .. .. | 24 |
| ,, | enlistment.. .. .. .. .. .. .. .. | 25 |
| ,, | post at the Conservatoire .. .. .. .. .. | 25 |
| ,, | letters to his wife.. .. .. .. .. .. .. | 28 |
| ,, | imbroglio with NAPOLEON .. .. .. .. | 30, 36, 37 |
| ,, | " Deux Journées " period .. .. .. .. | 31—35 |
| ,, | " Journal d'Apollon " .. .. .. : .. .. | 35, 36 |
| ,, | visit to Vienna .. .. .. .. .. .. .. | 39 |
| ,, | meeting with NAPOLEON .. .. .. .. .. | 40 |
| ,, | business speculations .. .. .. .. .. .. | 40 |
| ,, | return to Paris .. .. .. .. .. .. .. | 41 |
| ,, | card-drawing craze .. .. .. .. .. .. | 42 |
| ,, | nervous illness .. .. .. .. .. .. .. | 43 |
| ,, | visit to the CHIMAY family .. .. .. .. .. | 44 |
| ,, | beginning as a Church composer .. .. .. .. | 44 |
| ,, | regret for HAYDN.. .. .. .. .. .. .. | 45 |
| ,, | hymn for HAYDN .. .. .. .. .. .. .. | 45 |
| ,, | work in 1814 .. .. .. .. .. .. | 47—49 |
| ,, | fortunes under the Restoration.. .. .. .. | 49, 55 |
| ,, | connection with the Philharmonic Society .. .. | 49, 52 |
| ,, | second visit to London .. .. .. .. .. | 50—54 |
| ,, | offer from Berlin .. .. .. .. .. .. .. | 53 |
| ,, | return to Paris .. .. .. .. .. .. .. | 55 |
| ,, | appointment as chapel-master .. .. .. .. .. | 56 |
| ,, | good nature .. .. .. .. .. .. | 60—62 |
| ,, | relations with his fellow-musicians .. .. .. | 60—70 |
| ,, | works from 1814 to 1822 .. .. .. .. .. | 70 |
| ,, | appointment to the Directorship of the Conservatoire .. | 72 |
| ,, | " artistic honesty " .. .. .. .. .. | 73—75 |
| ,, | last compositions.. .. .. .. .. .. .. | 78 |
| ,, | retirement .. .. .. .. .. .. .. .. | 82 |
| ,, | death .. .. .. .. .. .. .. .. | 85 |
| ,, | funeral .. .. .. .. .. .. .. | 86, 87 |

| | PAGE |
|---|---|
| " Demetrio " | 10 |
| " Démophon " | 13, 16—19 |
| Desfaucherets | 31 |
| Desriaux | 16 |
| " Deux Journées, Les " | 31—34 |
| " Elise " | 24 |
| " Emma " | 31 |
| " Epicure " | 35 |
| " Estelle " | 14 |
| " Faniska " | 40 |
| Felicis, The | 4 |
| " Festivals of Youth and Gratitude, The " | 26 |
| " Finta Principessa, La " | 11 |
| " Giulio Sabini " | 11 |
| Halévy on Cherubini | 6, 14—16, 18 |
| Hiller and Cherubini | 65 |
| Hoche " Pompe Funèbre," The | 29 |
| Hoffmann | 26 |
| " Hôtellerie Portugaise, L'" | 30 |
| " Idalide L'" | 9 |
| " Ifigenia in Aulide " | 14 |
| *Journal d'Apollon, Le* | 35 |
| Jouy, M. | 47 |
| " Koukourgi " | 24 |
| " Lamentations of Jeremiah " | 5 |
| Legros | 12 |
| Léonard | 19 |
| Leopold, Duke | 7 |
| Lesueur | 39, 56 |
| " Lodoiska " | 21—23 |
| Louis, M. | 24, 28 |
| Marchesi | 9 |
| " Mariage de Salomon " | 70 |
| Marmontel | 16, 18 |
| Mass in F, The | 44 |
| " Médée " | 25—27 |
| Mendouze | 38 |
| Messenzio | 8 |
| " Nausicaa " | 47 |

| | PAGE |
|---|---|
| PAISIELLO | 37 |
| " PIMMALIONÈ " | 46 |
| " PUBLICA, FELICITÀ, LA " | 5 |
| " PUNITION, LA " | 31 |
| | |
| QUARTET in E FLAT, The | 49 |
| „ „ C, The | 81 |
| QUINTET, The | 82 |
| " QUINTO, FABIO, IL " | 8 |
| | |
| RECORDS of CHERUBINI'S BIRTH | 2 |
| " REPUBLICAN ODE " | 26 |
| " REQUIEM," The | 57 |
| ROSSINI and CHERUBINI | 64, 83 |
| | |
| SALPÊTRE RÉPUBLICAIN, LE " | 26 |
| SARETTE | 25, 49 |
| SARTI | 7, 8 |
| " SPOSO DI TRE, LA " | 9 |
| | |
| THÉÂTRE DE MONSIEUR, The | 20 |
| „ FEYDEAU | 21 |
| TOUG, M. | 47 |
| TOURETTE, Mdlle. | 24 |
| | |
| VIOTTI | 12, 20, 71 |
| VOGEL | 16 |